P9-BZB-171

#15 **ROUGH TRADE**

JOSEPH MEEK

PINNACLE BOOKS
WINDSOR PUBLISHING CORP.

PINNACLE BOOKS are published by

Windsor Publishing Corp.
475 Park Avenue South
New York, NY 10016

First Printing: October, 1993

Printed in the United States of America

WARRIOR KILL

Pike glared about him at the charging Blackfeet braves, his set jaw hard, one big hand gripping his Green River knife, the other the tomahawk that always stood him in good stead.

The nearest warrior, a giant almost the mountain man's own size, ran in hard, the muscles in his bare chest rippling, his war club raised for a bone-smashing blow.

But Jack sidestepped the savage and the club hit air not flesh. Then, he retaliated with a quick, hard tomahawk chop, burying the deadly blade in the Indian's skull. Blood mixed with gray matter as the red man fell, the shriek of agony dying in his throat as he hit the ground.

DEDICATION:

To Marilyn, who's now really on top . . .

Prologue

I

The night on the high prairie was dark, so dark that the wiry little cavalryman's surroundings down in the creek gully seemed painted in ink. The soles of his boots crunched streamside gravel as he edged blindly forward, guided by the water's gurgling sound.

Christ, thought Orlo Brubaker, scratching his armpit through his shirt of regulation blue. *This is spooky—blacker'n the inside of a witch's twat.*

Orlo wanted—needed—to make contact with the man he'd made his deal with. In another hour the moon would rise, making it harder to return unseen to his sentry post. The other lookouts stationed around the bivouac might be bored, but they couldn't all be counted on to be completely careless. Damn Captain Leland and his harsh discipline! The army party was a spit-and-polish unit, forged and vigilant.

It had been pure hell, setting up tonight's theft of army guns and ammo. But Orlo, a buck private on the remuda detail, had managed. At this moment, a hundred yards back, stood picketed two sturdy pack animals laden with muskets, powder, government-issue paper-cased cartridges. The muskets could be sold for fifty– to one-hundred dollars apiece—to mountain men at any of a dozen trading posts.

The man he only knew as Milt—whom he'd met only twice, the week before when the troop had ridden in company with a wagon train for three whole days—had offered to buy whatever number of army guns Orlo could steal from his fellow soldiers. The money offered was—in Orlo's eyes—considerable: twenty dollars per musket, no less. Of course that figure was nothing compared to what Milt stood to make in profits when he took the plunder around to the Rocky Mountain trading posts and converted it to cash.

Eventually, according to Orlo's vague plan, he'd desert, join forces with Milt and embark on a great carouse. Why, back in St. Louis there'd be whiskey and whores enough to keep their peckers up for months to come. .. . .

"Hist! Orlo, is that y'all?" The army thief couldn't see his partner in crime, but he recognized his voice.

"Yeah, Milt, it's me!" Orlo called back, softly.

A shadowy form ghosted up. "Where-at's them guns?"

"Back up the trail. Tied on pack hosses. I'll go fetch 'em now."

A low chuckle. "You do that, friend. I'll be a-waitin' right here."

Orlo turned, began retracing his steps. Leaving the

animals back there while he'd walked ahead to make the contact—it hadn't been a bad idea. Some of the footing was tricky. Now up again on the flat, he began to hotfoot it with long, quick strides. The worst thing possible was for a horse to slip, break a leg maybe, leave no way to transport those guns . . .

A loud voice rasped at Orlo in the night: "Halt! Stand where you are! This is Sergeant O'Dell! Six cavalrymen have you in their muskets' sights!"

"Don't shoot! I ain't goin' nowheres!" But Orlo Brubaker's legs itched to run. He couldn't keep them from running. He stretched them in long strides, starting to flee headlong!

A crunch of footfalls behind him seemed to be gaining. In the darkness, shadowy forms were closing in. Then Orlo was grabbed by six or eight hands that dragged at him. He tried to fight back, but was punched in his abdomen and kidneys till he was knocked down.

"Goddamn y'all, ain't takin' this coon!"

"Oh no, Private Brubaker?" The gruff voice belonged to O'Dell.

Stiff leather boottoes thudded into Orlo. Pain blossomed in his body and squeezed his skull. "Y'aint takin' me! Me'n my pard, we almost pulled it off . . . Almost."

A kick inpacted the private's head. A wave of agony exploded in his skull.

Orlo Brubaker felt he was whirling down . . . down.

And then there was nothing.

The next morning, fifty miles to the north, two mountain men were breaking the camp they'd spent the night in beside a tinkling, burbling stream. Jack Pike and his good friend Skins McConnell were in need of supplies, and so were heading for the Fort Laramie trading station—*not* as yet a military post—at the juncture of several age-old Indian trails. Pike, six-feet-four-inches tall and two-hundred-forty pounds of solid bone and muscle, jerked his saddle from the ground, threw it effortlessly on the back of his big gray gelding.

McConnell was asking him: "How long you figure it, Jack? About another day?"

"Another day'll do it, Skins."

"Y'know, Jack, I aim to lay off demon rum. Something I promised myself over the winter trapping season. Rum's no good for a man's stomach." Through his fringed buckskin shirt he rubbed his middle. Behind him stood his saddled blaze-faced bay mount, patient as ever.

"No good for a man's stomach?"

"Not at all."

Pike grinned. "How about a woman's stomach, then? What about that?"

Skins puzzled, then shrugged. "That isn't for me to decide. All I'm telling you is, no more rum for me. No more full bottles, not so much as a swig."

"Because the stuff's no good for a man's stomach?"

"That's true. Entirely true."

Both men glanced around the campsite they were leaving. Then they swung aboard their horses and gigged them forward. West. After almost a half-mile, Pike said, "Y'know, it'll be a change, Skins. You not getting drunk."

His friend looked at him hard. "Not getting drunk? What gave you that notion—that I'll not get drunk?"

Pike frowned. "But you just said . . ."

"What I said was, I'd given up rum. I never said I was through with beer. Or whiskey. Or brandy. Or wine."

Pike, tall in the saddle, laughed. "You're a caution, Skins, and there's no arguing with you. I know that."

McConnell, meanwhile, hadn't stopped talking. "Or sangaree from the islands. Or punch from foreign shores. Pike, you reckon the saloon at Laramie sells punch?"

The horsemen rode on.

The sun scaled up the morning sky, and the dew began to dry from the tall, golden buffalo grass . . .

Chapter 1

"You're a damned sucker if you go over there, pard," Jack Pike remarked to Skins McConnell as the pair strolled the adobe-walled courtyard of Fort Laramie.

"Aw, but Jack, I been up in them mountains for months! No likker, no women, no *fun!* So damn it, I aim to investigate this."

"Well, if you've got your mind set as a mossy-horned old buffalo bull . . . ."

"That's the point, Jack! I've got my mind set, so c'mon and tag along whilst I go kick up my heels a little!"

Pike fell in step behind his friend. But as the big mountain man strode the compound, he raked his sandy beard with his fingers and wagged his head. When McConnell wanted things his way, sometimes humoring him seemed in order. This appeared to be one of those times.

He let his lanky friend lead him through the crowd of buckskin-clad trappers, the clerks wearing manufactured clothes from back East, the soldiers in their blue uniforms. Also roaming the compound were a large number of Indian bucks and squaws—peaceable Brule Sioux come to trade for beads, cloth and other white man's goods.

All these people McConnell shouldered past, making a bee-line for a slouch-shouldered man in frock coat and top hat. The coat was frayed at the sleeves. The owner, who stood behind a small, waist-high portable table, looked to be his early forties. His mustache drooped, and so did his eyelids.

The cave-chested scarecrow was calling out: "Try your luck, gents! See which is faster, the hand or the eye! Try your luck!"

As the gambler droned his come-on, his smooth, paste-white hands never rested. Around and around the small tabletop they glided swiftly, sliding three polished walnut shells.

"Under which shell resides the pea, gents? Place your bet and take your pick!"

Oh, no groaned Pike inwardly. *The old shell game. Don't fall for this, McConnell! Not when we could be inside, bellying it up to the bar, swigging down brew. Just so long as it isn't rum . . .*

But McConnell's look had hardened into determination. And everything he'd said was true—he *had* worked hard all winter up in the beaver valley. The harvest of pelts the pair had packed down a few weeks ago now lay, dried and tanned, in the storerooms of the post.

And after all the cold, the toil, the loneliness, maybe a man *was* entitled to some fun.

But, Pike wondered, was it actually fun to part with one's hard-earned money? The gambler wore a decidedly shady look.

Well, To each his own, Pike thought, keeping his mouth shut for now.

Holding his long, heavy rifle—Hawken Brothers, St. Louis—in his left hand, he let his right hand rest on the bone haft of his sheathed Green River knife. He let his alert, sharp eyes scan past the gambler and the milling crowd, closed his ears to all the jabbering voices and the clanging of hammers at the blacksmith forge. A string of laden pack horses moved past, churning dust. A mongrel barked.

To Pike there seemed but one good thing about where the gambler stood: it was out of the sun. Three sides of the post's quadrangle consisted of buildings which were set against the outer walls, their roofs forming walkways and parapets. Behind the gambler's stand loomed the fourth side, a thick, fifteen-foot wall. Now, in this late afternoon of a warm spring day, the band of shade it flung was welcome.

McConnell edged forward confidently, his own Hawken slung over his shoulder on a thong. In his right hand he now held a coin. "All right, mister shell-man . . . I'm here to match your moves an' put my money where my mouth is. I'm bettin' this silver dollar on my peepers!"

"You're on, good sir!" snapped the gambling professional. Then he added: "Melody, gal . . . Hold this sportsman's bet." A woman Pike hadn't noticed before turned, flashed a bright smile, held out a small, soft hand. McConnell crossed her palm with silver.

14

Why Pike hadn't noticed her right off was a puzzle. She'd been standing half-concealed behind the gambler, but she was the loveliest creature Pike had seen for months. The woman was not only pretty in the face, but well-formed of body. She wore a scoop-necked dress of powder blue, and the garment did little conceal her ample charms. Her waist was tiny, and farther up, high, prominent breasts stretched the fabric.

"Sir, what about you? Do *you* wish to place a wager?" She flashed sparkling topaz eyes at the big mountain man.

"No, I don't reckon so."

The gambler briefly lifted each of his shells in turn, dropped a little dried pea on the table, then covered it. He commenced sliding the shells around, faster and faster, till both hands and shells moved in a blur of speed. Then all at once, they stopped. "There, pick a shell!" he barked.

"That one." Skins pointed to his pick.

"A winner! It's your lucky day, sir. Melody, pay the man."

McConnell said, "No, hold the money . . . I'm gonna play some more. Double my bet! Here's another silver cartwheel."

"All right, then, we'll go again." The frock-coated man's hands sped and stopped. McConnell chose again, again he guessed right. "Another try, another win!"

Skins glanced at Pike, who stood by wearing an amused expression. "Don't want any action? It's all mine? Then, let 'er ride again," Skins told Melody. "But add this five dollars from my pocket to the pot!"

15

The money glittering in her hands, the young woman beamed. Also smiling was the shell-game man. People in the crowd who'd noted the excitement drifted over to stand near Pike and McConnell in their long-fringed buckskins and neck-slung powder horns. Other trappers converged, also clad in fringed buckskins and neck-slung powder horns. These men, plus the traders and army men, braves and squaws, formed a wide half-circle. Pike and McConnell leaned on rifles, their sharp gaze fixed on those speeding, shifty shells.

The shells stopped, and the gambler's hands dropped to his sides. "So where's the pea?"

"D'you think you know, Skins?" Pike asked.

"I don't think I know, I *know* I know! I kept my eyes peeled. Never so much as blinked!"

The crowd's low murmurings became a loud buzz. "Point 'er out, fella!" whooped a corporal.

"Make it quick," cried the blacksmith. "My forge is gettin' cold."

"There!" Skins crowed.

The shell gamester lifted the shell pointed at.

Nothing.

Nothing but the foot-square tabletop! Skins McConnell stood dumbfounded. "Damn! I thought . . .''

Then a yell was raised, back in the crowd. "T'ain't no surprise, mister. 'Handy' Hooper, ol' slick-as-a-whistle, he's a damn cheat!"

A trapper in greasy buckskins shouldered forward. "Handy Hooper," he growled, "lets a fella win a-purpose for a while. Each play the sucker bets a little more. But, y'see, Handy palms the pea, maybe tucks it

16

up his sleeve. Why, he cleaned *me* out yesterday! A whole winter's worth a pelts lost, damn the bastard!''

The angry black-beard plowed from the pack, kicked aside the table, drew a knife. His voice lifted to a roar. "I, Willy Webb's a-gonna kill ya, Hooper!''

Then Jack Pike swung into action, letting fall his Hawken and doubling his fists. His massive frame moving between attacker and attacked, Pike lashed out with a fist. His knuckles sledged Willy Webb's chest. The diversion let Hooper slip away in the crowd.

"Yer standin' up fer that crook?'' Willy Webb's demented eyes blazed. He charged Pike then, the sun glinting on his blade.

Pike dodged the stab, then retaliated, his fist darting under the knife blade. He slammed down his arm, and the knife went spinning. Willy Webb kept coming, but only ran into an uppercut. The bearded chin flattened and blood flowed from the trapper's split lip.

And then he toppled.

Members of the crowd shouted and slapped each others' backs. "Didja see it?''

"Cold-cocked 'im in one punch!''

Pike hissed to Skins, "Come on, let's get out of here.''

"You're right. Our work here's done.'' Then Hooper's female partner caught his eye. "Jack, what about the gal?''

Pike took the redhead's arm. "Want to come with us, miss? The crowd could get ugly.''

"Why, much obliged, for your protection, Mister . . . ?''

"Pike. Just call me Pike.''

But his words were drowned by tumult. The hub-bub was boiling as someone yelled: "Webb got knocked out, but the blame was Hooper's. Say, where *is* Hooper, the low shell-game cheat?"

"I've a sleeping room rented in one the build-ings," Pike told the woman. "A quiet place."

"Sounds nice."

Melody, Pike and Skins went inside, where the massive ceiling beams almost brushed Pike's head. McConnell peeled off, seeming hell-bent for the mess hall and its crude bar.

"Hey, Skins," Pike said. "How about the quar-ters?"

McConnell shook his head. "First I got to have a drink." He grinned sheepishly. "Gambling's thirsty work."

The woman thrust out Skins's money. "First take back this. I'm sorry for what happened out there. There's an explanation I'll tell you sometime."

"No explanation needed, Melody. Thanks anyhow."

By now Pike was leading the woman to a staircase. McConnell wasn't going; he'd seen "that look" in Pike's eyes.

"That look" was the hot look, a look that signaled "two's company, but three's a crowd."

"Well, on to the saloon," McConnell muttered. "I got deciding to do—whiskey or rum? Maybe Taos lightning?"

Then he pumped his gun high and grinned. "I got it—I'm having me Albuquerque beer!"

Chapter 2

The interior of the room Pike had rented for a few days was small, with crumbling adobe hung with threadbare trade blankets. The furniture was sparse: just a washstand and an old rope bed. Light came from a window, at this warm season the shutters were flung wide. On this, the second storey, the noise drifting up from the courtyard seemed faint.

"Well," Pike said. "Here we are, safe. That crowd doesn't cotton to shell-game cheats. They'll be hunting for that fella, Handy Hooper. And next thing you know, someone'll remember his female pard."

The woman sighed, brushed a loose tendril of red hair from her forehead. "Handy's my older brother, Mr. Pike, and what a wastrel. That's why he brought me out West—to try and recoup the family fortune he'd lost by his gaming ways. Oh, the money went on racehorses, cards, dice—you name it. But the last thousand dollars slipped away too, and we were reduced to . . . to what you saw in the yard."

A sob tugged at her pretty throat. "Handy would

19

simply tell me to stand by his side and look pretty, then proceed to cheat whoever he was playing with. He's able to palm the pea, hide it up his sleeve." The topaz orbs grew large and tear-misted. "Oh, Mr. Pike, I'm so ashamed! If I only knew an honest way I might earn a living."

Pike shrugged. "Well it doesn't appear you're the crooked one in the family. Maybe something can be done. Right now you need to stay calm. Why not set a while, just make yourself comfortable?"

Demurely, she sat on the bed. The grass-stuffed mattress sank beneath her weight. She was a slip of a gal, but healthy as well as good looking, Pike mused.

"So your name's Melody Hooper?"

She bestowed her smile. "That's me. Now look here, Mr. Pike . . ."

"Like I said a while ago downstairs, Melody, just plain Pike'll do betwixt you and me. I don't care much for name handles."

"Pike, then. What I was about to say was, what you did down there saved my brother's life. He managed to slip away in the fuss, but I have no doubt he's still nearby. He has no way of leaving Fort Laramie. But I promise you, I'm through with dishonest ways. I've decided to sell my mother's ring. The small amount I get will pay my way to Richmond."

"You've family back there?"

"Yes. But it may be too late to raise the money today, and book passage too. Evening's coming on." The sunset was indeed a pretty one. Through the window it could be seen, all vermilion and gold.

In the golden light the woman had a seductive look—decidedly seductive. "I'll make travel plans tomorrow," she recapped, "but, Pike, what do you suggest we do now?"

Pike stood his Hawken in the corner by the bedstead. "*We* do? You and me? Melody, are you hinting at something?"

"You guessed it, Pike. I'm so grateful for what you've done, I think I owe you a reward."

Then she was off the bed and into his arms, the mountain man reacting, pressing his mouth to hers. She kissed him back, firmly. Melody's lips writhed and her tongue probed. Her hands fluttered up and down the mountain man's back. Then she broke the lip-lock. "I want you, Pike. Lordy, how I want you. You look like the answer to my dream, to any gal's dream!"

He acknowledged it. "Yeah, I reckon I can take care of a woman's needs."

"Then, for God's sake, *do it!*"

Her warm breathing gusted against Pike's neck as his strong fingers found her narrow waist. Melody squirmed in his arms, enjoying his touch, but also tugging at her buttons and bows. As soon as Pike discovered she was disrobing, his penis started straining his buckskins.

A whisper of fabric, and the woman's clothes fell around her ankles. With a trim bare foot she kicked them free. Her lusciously curved body and slender legs caused a flood of arousal to rush through Pike's loins. His eyes feasted on the woman's nakedness—especially her round, firm breasts, crested with strawberry-sized nubbins. The areolas were a dark pink, puckered and dollar-sized. Her bountiful upper body tapered downward, filling to satiny, lush, cream-white hips. A nap of reddish curls matted the triangle at her come-together.

The sight made Pike's stalk lift even higher, stiffer.

He began shedding buckskins, with Melody's eager help. Her fingers flew to undo the lacings, then tugged the shirt over his head and shoved down his trousers. By the time he stood nude, his engorged phallus was as hard as a rail-spike. It's silky foreskin felt about to burst, and the woman's eyes popped at the splendid vision.

Pike, over the years, had had occasion to do battle, and he showed the marks of them. The pale inden-tations on his skin, the worm-like darker scars caught Melody's attention. But only for a minute or so, for no woman could ignore his rigid instrument. Melody felt weak at the sight of the erect pole, the pouching treasure sack.

She blinked excitedly, stretched her hand out to touch his tool. Her palm expertly caressed his male gristle. Pike used both hands to clasp Melody's waist, to pull her warm and willing body to him.

He lowered her to the grass mattress, then dropped next to her. Investigating her body, he dropped his head, his nose sniffing the heady fragrance where her thighs joined.

Seeing her pink puffiness there, he glued his lips to her crotch and feasted. The woman gave a low moan of ecstasy.

With his tongue, he parted her folds and her hot

juices bathed his taste buds. Pike continued to ply his tongue, and was rewarded by more delectable nectar.

"Oh, Pike. Oh, Pike," the woman groaned. "I want you in me—but let me play it my way, at least just once?"

Then she was no longer on her back, but rearranging her position and swinging above him. On all fours, she straddled the man's big frame, her own body shuddering as much as his. As she lowered herself, his enormous organ brushed her pliant lower swell. Then she sat, mounted atop his stalk, guiding his curved length deep into her hot love chamber.

His tender rod-tip throbbed at contact with her passage, which contracted exquisitely as she took him in. Her tiny joy–button swelled and pulsed, and Pike, guessing her need, began to stroke vigorously. Melody mewed, every nerve-end a-tingle. Pike lunged violently, to her delight.

Christ, it's good, Pike thought.

As for Melody: *If it kills me, it kills me! What better way to die?* she wondered.

Pike thrusted again and again deeper into the woman, while she in turn rode, bucking and quaking, to match his moves. A syrupy flow leaked from where their bodies' joined: the inevitable was coming fast. The woman frantically rocked and rolled, milking pleasure at the same time she gave it. With each stroke Pike delved to the hilt, Melody gasping each time he nudged her womb's mouth.

For a while all of Pike's thoughts fled. Forgotten was Handy Hooper, McConnell, even the mountain men's upcoming trapping venture. For Pike the sexual pleasure was peaking. Sensation raged.

The interlocked pair climaxed simultaneously. The mutual sensations flowed and ebbed, two shuddering bodies in the growing dusk. Finally Melody stopped rocking, hiked a shapely leg and dropped from his come-slick rod.

"I was expecting the spectacular, Pike," she murmured. "But that was more than spectacular—it was terrific."

"I know the feeling," he rasped. They clung to each other like nestling spoons, their breathing growing relaxed as their heartbeats slowed.

A quarter-hour later, Pike's tongue re-ignited her blaze. This time Melody lay back, allowing Pike to use his magic wand. As he buried his manhood into her seething channel, the woman's cauldron overflowed—and then some.

She whimpered and convulsed as he plowed her furrow, and screamed in ecstasy as he hosed her depths.

Chapter 3

It was the morning of the next day, and Pike lay with Melody atop the old rope bed. She had slipped his buckskin shirt on—a garment with sleeves—and was showing the mountain man how a shell-game artist could conceal a dried pea between his fingers, transfer it to his shirt cuff, and produce it again when needed.

"So you see, Pike," she was saying, "my gambler brother is like a magician, in a way. The hand is quicker than the eye, but it's also said a practitioner's nerve's behind the hand. Now watch, and I'll show you the moves again."

She'd been carrying a set of three shells in a dress pocket—Handy's spares, she'd explained—and now she moved them around on the bed quilt. "Of course, how you move the shells isn't really the trick. I mean, if the pea's not under *any* of them, there's no way the sucker can win. Here, you try it."

"I'm buck-naked, Melody. I've got no shirt or sleeve."

"True. But you don't really need sleeves, either. Here, let me show you how to hide the pea between your fingers and fool the ones you're betting against."

She leaned forward and Pike could see, under the shirt, those large breasts of hers. Pike made a grab for her. She permitted herself be caught, permitted the shirt be pulled over her head and leave her naked. Entering into the playful spirit, she took hold of Pike's burgeoning penis. She employed her hand pumping him, and surges of pleasure shot through the mountain man.

He licked his lips and grunted.

"Feel good, Pike? I want you again—even after all we've had! But first, I think I'll just drive you a bit crazy."

But before things went farther this time, their ears picked up the sounds of a commotion outside. "Damn!" The mountain man knelt on the bed, cast his gaze through the window to scan the yard.

The courtyard seemed filled with blue. Dirty-shirt blue, with lots and lots of rank chevrons.

The United States Army had arrived!

A whole party of them!

Oh, there were other people in the compound beside the soldiers, Pike saw the usual mix of trappers, traders, Indians. But today the military was the show, its focus an officer wearing captain's shoulderboards. He stood in the midst of his men—tall, blond-mustached and ramrod-straight. He spoke to a lieutenant, who passed the order to a sergeant, who bawled out: "All right men. Ten-*shun!*"

Immediately, the heels of nearly thirty soldiers

26

clicked together as they came to attention. All the kepi bills pointed full-front, the eyes under them straight ahead.

Under one arm, the sergeant carried a long, coiled whip.

"Bring out Orlo Brubaker." he called. "Bind the prisoner to the stake."

Pike's gaze took in the tall whipping post that had been planted almost at the compound's center. An iron ring was embedded near the top. Two troopers now marched grimly toward it, and between them stumbled a guilty-looking, swarthy man. The poor wretch's wrists were secured in iron manacles.

"Who's that?" Melody asked. "What's going on?"

"Army stuff," Pike said with disgust. "Looks like we're about to see a flogging."

This surprised her. "But, why have it here?"

Pike pondered a minute, then ventured an opinion. "Oh, it's true Laramie's a trading post, and not a military post. But what else *is* there, out on the lone prairie? Fort Union, back down the Oregon Trail, is a long way off." He paused, then: "Melody, some soldier boy's got himself in hot water—likely broke a regulation or two. Those officers, they can be ornery bastards."

"Private Brubaker, get set to receive your punishment. Sergeant O'Dell, prepare the prisoner."

A brisk salute. "Yessir!"

Brubaker, his face bruised and his eyes glazed, didn't resist. He was stripped to the waist, exposing a scrawny bronze torso, and then the corporals flung him against the post. They lashed his wrist chains to the ring, so Orlo's arms were pulled above his head and stretched achingly. His groin ached, too, where he'd been kicked in the nuts to wake him from a fitful sleep.

So close to makin' the big haul, too, Orlo was thinking. *Gettin' caught was a bad break if'n there ever was one. And all them muskets, all back in the sojers' hands!*

Milt had gotten away clean, but a lot of good that did Orlo. The man with the ideas would never again opt for Orlo as his pard. From now on, Orlo would be known as a man who'd been flogged for stealing army property.

Flogged?

Oh, Jesus! They really aim to do it to me!

The ramrod-straight captain called out again. "Prisoner, have you any words to say? Perhaps name the civilian accomplice who would have fenced the stolen property?"

Orlo spat, and followed it with a gutteral Indian phrase.

"Sergeant, do your duty."

"Happy to, sir!"

The sergeant planted his feet and shook out the lash—all fourteen feet of wicked blacksnake. The thing lay in the dirt, seeming to squirm as if alive. The whipman's eyes had started to glitter, bright and hard. Suddenly his hand exploded into lightning motion, sending the long whip licking out viciously. The braided leather hissed and snapped, and the lash tore into Brubaker's thin back.

Thwack!

Orlo, despite attempts to steel himself, winced. The pain jolted him. And now the whip came at him again, from the side this time, to gouge a welt across his shoulder blades. The man vented a gasp. Again and again the lash fell, and each stroke seared Orlo like strokes of a red-hot brush. He felt his skin tear as the sergeant worked the instrument, laying a ladder pattern along his bare skin.

Finally a vicious swipe split the skin, and Orlo jerked at his bonds like a hooked sturgeon. O'Dell kept dealing blows. Orlo bit his lips till blood trickled at their corners. His eyes bugged each time the whip fell, and his body twitched. The crimson liquid lines across his back multiplied. The man spat out more threats in the tongue of the Blackfeet.

Two hard strokes later, Orlo's scream broke the hot morning air.

From his perch in the blockhouse window, Pike glanced from the flogging victim to the army captain. The officer's mouth moved each time the lash struck. Reading the lips, the mountain man guessed he was counting.

Slowly the victim's back became a lacerated mess. He'd be wearing scars for the rest of his life. Now, with each stroke of the lash came a scream and a shower of blood droplets that spotted nearby uniforms. But the disciplined soldiers didn't flinch. They didn't dare to.

Then O'Dell spoke. "He's about finished, Captain Leland, sir."

"He hasn't received the thirty lashes assigned. Carry on, sergeant!"

"Yessir!"

More strokes and flying blood drops followed, but the screams were now losing volume. The private slumped from his wrists, his legs like jelly, his whole body slack.

"That makes thirty strokes," Leland shouted. "Enough! Cut the man down and sluice his back with salt water. The rest of you men are dis-*missed!*" The troopers broke ranks and trudged off, except for those assigned to take care of the prisoner. Captain Leland ambled off with two lieutenants, the officers adjourning to a tent outside the gate.

Up in the room, Melody Hooper turned to Pike. The woman's face was slightly greenish.

"Pike, after watching, er, that—Well, I just don't feel much like . . ."

"I know what you mean. I don't either." The mountain man grabbed his trousers and pulled them on. He shoved his feet into tough, elk-hide moccasins. When his shirt covered his muscle-slabbed chest, and his powder horns were slung, he turned to the woman and said, "I'm going down there."

"I guessed," Melody replied. "And I've business of my own to tend to. This is the day I'll sell my heirloom ring. Buy my way back East with the next pack train, Pike. There ought to be one leaving in a day or two. No use trying to persuade my brother to go—he won't. Oh, he'll get caught cheating eventually, and when he does . . ."

Pike studied the woman, as he enjoyed doing. "I figure we both hope the same thing for Handy. That nothing like a whipping ever befalls him. Maybe he'll reform one of these days.''

"Well, gal, be seeing you later.'' The mountain man picked up his rifle, headed for the stairs.

"Meantime, Pike, I'll be thinking of you,'' Melody sighed. "And my memory's big and strong, just like that cock that's meant so much to me!''

Chapter 4

After leaving Melody in the sleeping—and screwing—room, Pike wandered to the taproom. There, as expected, he ran into McConnell. His friend was in the midst of a shoulder-to-shoulder crowd of noisy drinkers. When Pike spoke, he had to bellow over the din. "Did you catch this morning's entertainment?"

"Couldn't miss it," Skins said. "Could anyone?"

Pike signaled for a brew, and across the pine-plank bar came a foaming stein. Quaffing off the head, the big man remarked, "By the way, that jasper that got flogged, d'you know his offense?"

"That's a secret," McConnell said.

"Secret?"

"So they say. No civilian I've talked to seems to have the information. As for the soldier-boys, they're not talking."

"You don't say?" McConnell saw Pike look around, mischief in his eyes.

"Now, hold on a minute, Jack. I don't like it when you get that look."

The soldier Pike walked up to was a mere private—the lowest of the low. He couldn't have been much older than eighteen. Although his cavalry blouse was brushed and the buttons polished, the kid's chin was weak and his posture gangly. Unless Pike missed his guess he was a recruit, with less than six months in the service. "Friend," Pike said, throwing his arm around the kid, "you look almost too dry to spit. Can I buy you a drink?"

"Well-l-l, ya ain't an army man. Got some connection with us sojers?"

"Nope."

"Mister, I don't know ya from Adam."

"Now you do. Name's Jack Pike."

"Oh, what the hell—sure I'll let ya treat Mel Crank. Mel Crank, that's me." The kid shuffled his booted feet in the sawdust on the floor. "Ain't got many friends, far's I be from m'home in Alabam."

"So, what'll you have, lad?"

"Er, whiskey? Can you afford a glass of the stuff?"

"Hang the cost!" Pike slapped two bits on the bar, and the drink was shoved across. "You hail from Alabama, you say? Nice country, for being back in the East."

A timid grin from the kid. "The West, it sure is different. Scary. Hell, there's all that wilderness out there, and were goin' out into it, just a party of 'bout thirty sojers."

The mountain man raised his glass. "Here's to the fella who took the whipping this morning!"

The private gagged on his booze, drooled some

down his chin and sprayed the rest through his lips. "Mister, I cain't drink t' that."

Pike glanced at Skins, who stood grinning, then back to the kid. "You won't drink the drink I bought you?"

"Er . . ."

"I can't hear you!"

The room was low-ceilinged and dim, and if anything, the shouting and bar-slapping was even noisier than a few minutes ago. The mob at the bar was three deep.

"I said, I can't hear you!"

"N-no! I c-can't drink with y'all!"

Pike shouted at the private standing beside the first private. "Did you hear what this pipsqueak told me? That he won't drink up, after I bought him whiskey!"

This was another greenhorn enlistee. "Whyn't ya shove off an' leave us be, mister? This is our first day off in weeks. We sure don't need no trouble with the sarge."

"I'm gonna bust your friend in the nose!" Pike was faking rage and doing it well.

"No, don't do that!"

Pike and McConnell had maneuvered the young men toward a log wall away from the other army men, the hard-looking veterans who looked as if they could fight white men or redskin hostiles. Trappers and clerks made up the throng in this corner. One of the kids went for his sidearm, albeit hesitantly. "No gunplay, Lester," his companion blurted.

"The sarge?"

"Sure, the sarge. He'll have our asses in a sling."

Pike kept needling the pair. "Well, who's gonna tell me what I want to know?" Pike's manner was mean, and his voice was meaner. "What did the flogged man do wrong?"

"Got hisself whipped."

"I mean, *what offense did he commit?*"

The younger peach-fuzz-face broke first. "Shit ever'body in the outfit knows, so what's the hurt in your knowing? Private Brubaker, he stole him some guns—army guns. Two pack-horse loads. He's half-Injun, y'see and can't be trusted. Captain Leland, our commander, he figures Brubaker must've had a pard he was gonna sell the guns to. And the weapons would find their way to the ones who use 'em out in the West: mountain men. Say, you're a mountain man, mister. Would you've bought a stolen army musket?"

But Pike and McConnell had already turned on their heels and were striding toward the door. As soon as they were outside, they both sucked in lungfuls of clean, good air. "You hear what he told us?" Pike said.

"I heard."

Pike slapped his Hawken's stock below the flintlock. "I'd be damned leery of buying a musket from a fella as looks shady. And army muskets have army marks on 'em. The whipped man—Brubaker was he called? What if he'd managed to pull off his theft?"

"Tried for two pack-horses loaded with long guns. It must be like the soldier at the bar said, that he had somebody waiting to take 'em off his hands. Somebody stood to make a tidy profit. But with few or no white people dumb enough to buy what they'd for sure spot as army property . . . Say!'' Now the wheels in McConnell's brain were cranking. ''I heard Brubaker—when tied to the whipping post—spouting Indian talk! And it sounded like Blackfeet lingo!''

McConnell stood still in the yard and scratched his head. ''Pike, what if those guns found their way into the hands not of white men, but Indians?''

The big mountain man had an answer, and a grim one. ''Blackfeet bands armed not merely with tomahawks, bows, arrows—but with guns besides! Something new under Rocky Mountain skies!''

''Jesus!'' Skins was realizing the implications.

''Y'know,'' Pike was saying, ''that Brubaker fella might not take too well to punishment. Might rebound from it and carry a mean-streak grudge. What if he tries stealing guns again—and succeeds next time? Could be a bad Indian war!''

Chapter 5

Pike and McConnell spent some time that morning at the trading post's merchandise counters, buying gunpowder and lead for casting rifle balls, not to mention food like bacon by the slab and dried beans by the sackful. There were even some of Skins's personal favorites—raisins.

The hunting trip they were preparing for would use most of the goods, so they didn't think they were over-spending. Pike requested the items be put in burlap bags and kept ready. He told the clerk that he and Skins would pick the stuff up at daybreak, then load their pack horses and head out riding toward the northwest and the distant Tetons.

The mountain men ambled outside, and ignoring the Sioux bucks smoking their pipes and bantering with their women, decided to relax a bit in the morning sunshine. They leaned their rifles against the big old fur press, used for baling beaver pelts and buffalo robes.

But the mountain men weren't alone for long, for

a flat-faced, lean army man walked up, sleeve chevrons proclaiming him a sergeant. Pike recognized his face, but by then he was introducing himself. ''I believe you're the one called Mountain Jack Pike? I'm Sergeant O'Dell, United States Cavalry, at your service. I'm delivering a message, sir, from my commandant, Captain Maynard Leland. The captain requests the pleasure of meeting you and your friend. Immediately, if possible. In his tent.''

Pike pretended to think for a minute. Then, ''Well, if the captain's got a tent, why wouldn't it be possible to meet him in it? Can you see any reason not to, Skins?''

''Not so long as the tent's big enough.''

Not catching the humor, the noncom explained himself. ''I suppose I didn't make myself wholly clear. It was the 'immediately' part that raised the 'possible' point. The fact is, Mr. Pike, I'm here to summon you. *And* your friend, here. Now, if both you gentlemen would be so kind.''

''Well,'' McConnell said, grinning, ''I *am* pretty well known for my kind ways. I've been kind to puppy dogs, children and whores, mostly. As regards other critters, that all depends. Pike, about this kindness thing—you reckon I might qualify to see the captain?''

''Well, all things considered, Skins . . .''

''Gents,'' O'Dell snapped. ''I ain't got all day, so routine be damned. The Cap, he's got a proposition to put to you. Come and listen to it or go to hell—makes no difference to me!''

Pike eyed the sergeant. ''Y'know, sergeant, you're

starting to sound more like a sensible fella by the minute. like you're not a just a whip-swinging bully, after all.''

"I'm a noncom in this man's army, mister. That means giving orders sometimes, following 'em other times. Once in a while my superior officer orders an offender punished. I don't enjoy flogging men's backs, but sometimes a soldier deserves it. Orlo Brubaker deserved a flogging.''

"To nip his gun-running ways in the bud?''

O'Dell tugged at his gauntlet, looked at Pike with narrowed eyes. "You know about that, do you, Pike? Well, that reputation of yours may just be well founded. I've been told what the redskins call you.''

"He-Whose-Head-Touches-the-Sky,'' McConnell put in. "Yeah, that's what they call my big friend. And you'd better listen to 'em, sergeant. He's a rip-roaring, grizzly-whupper. Best Indianfighter there is in all the Rockies, and he knows more about the mountains than any other white man.''

Skins gestured at the peaks to be seen above the post walls. The slopes of the Laramie Range were green with cedar and pine. And the opposite direction, the three were aware, lay the Rockies—vast, threatening and filled with mystery. Pike knew much of what was out there, it was true, but not everything. The land was ripe for exploration, that was for sure.

"Well,'' O'Dell said, "come with me or not, whichever. As for me, I'll be reporting back to the captain.''

"This Captain Leland,'' Pike said inquiringly. "Why is he so far from the eastern forts, anyhow?

And what's a well-equipped army party, albeit a small one, doing in these parts? You don't have enough men to take on the hostile tribes."

"Ah, Pike, ain't you the curious one?" The sergeant cracked a sly grin. "Maybe it's the curiosity that'll lure you to the captain's tent."

Jack Pike sighed and shrugged. "Reckon we may as well go, take us a look-see and listen. C'mon, Skins, what's to be lost if we do?"

Inside the tent that Pike and McConnell were led to, they found the same three officers who'd left the post together after the flogging. There was also an older man, a civilian. They sat in camp chairs under the canvas peak, around a table spread with maps. All four rose at the entrance of the mountain men, the captain stepping forward to offer his hand, the two lieutenants seemingly waiting their turn.

"Thank you, gentlemen, for consenting to come. I'm Captain Maynard Leland, United States Army, and these are the other officers assigned to me on the present expedition. Lieutenant Gower Meester and Lieutenant Frederic Leland—who happens to be my son. Gentlemen, may I present Jack Pike and Skins McConnell, noted mountain men. They're the ones we've heard so much about since arriving here at Laramie."

"You know *my* name?" asked Skins, shaking hands.

"I heard first and most about your large friend, I must confess. But from what I've learned, I know you're close to Mr. Pike. That's why my offer regarding our mission includes you. Men, that offer is an invitation to join us. Before I go on to explain myself, may I present Mister Melchior Dix, of whom you may have heard. Mister Dix is an eminent scientist, late of Princeton, New Jersey.''

"Howdy, Mr. Dix. Lieutenants.''

"Howdy, Mr. Dix. Lieutenants,'' Skins parroted.

They were an interesting group. Leland senior was of medium height, and impeccably turned out in his tailor-made uniform. From flowing blond hair and mustache to boots of calfskin, Maynard Leland fit the image of a spit-and-polish career officer.

Son Frederic, in his twenties, was a slighter version his father, his uniform, too, obviously made by an expensive tailor. At least, at West Point, the young man had learned to dress. Lieutenant Meester was cut from different cloth, being lumpy-faced, squat and a bit shabby of uniform. When he shook hands he pursed his razor-slit mouth.

That left Melchior Dix, a tall, gangling man in his early sixties. His thick shock of hair had turned white—evidently from devoting himself to deep thoughts. The scientist also carried a somewhat harassed look—like the weight of the whole scientific community was on his shoulders.

Captain Leland smoothly guided the conversation. "Mr. Pike and Mr. McConnell, you must be wondering why I sent for you. Let me describe for you the nature of my command. When I introduced myself, I was incomplete—I belong to the Army Corps of Topographical Engineers. Our job is to map the

41

principle passes of the central Rockies, insofar as the mission can be carried out in one summer.''

Pike and McConnell exchanged glances. The bigger mountain man said, ''I don't see how . . .''

''How you'd fit in? Keep listening. Although the expedition is under the auspices of the military, its purpose isn't fighting. We want no Indian war. Our only purpose is to gather details for maps.''

Pike mused. ''I've heard tell about the stink being raised back in the capitol. The Oregon country is being opened up, and would-be settlers are demanding more and better routes there.''

''Ah, you *do* catch the political drift! Hear that Melchior? Fred? The man's catching the political drift!'' Captain Leland chuckled smugly. ''You're correct about the demand for routes, Pike, and the establishment of them, in turn, requires exploration! Only through exploration can the information be acquired to create the better maps we envision.''

The officer went on. ''Let me spell it out. These will be high-quality maps, the likes of which have never been seen before. Professor Dix has devised new and improved methods. Why, we've scientific instruments by the pack-horse load, consisting of navigation tools that—until now, Pike—have only been used by mariners at sea. We'll be plotting the latitude and longitude for every major landmark. And we'll also determine altitudes with utmost accuracy—by use of the barometer.''

''Well,'' Pike said, ''I can see the point, *up to* a point.'' He turned as if addressing Skins, although he knew McConnell already grasped his notions. ''Folks think today's maps of the frontier are jokes, made by men who've never even seen the places. Crooked lines stand for rivers, X-marks for mountains—and the distances between shown nowhere like they really are."

"All too true," Leland said. "That's the kind of thing we want to remedy!" He slapped the table so hard it swayed. "But what did you mean just now— you can see my point *up to a point?*"

Pike studied the group. Melchior Dix, young Fred Leland, even Captain Leland himself, all looked naively eager. The only exception was the older, somewhat hard-bitten Lieutenant Meester. The big mountain man pondered his response briefly, then began to talk. "Let me answer, captain, by asking a few questions. What experience have you or your men had with mountain travel? With mountain weather, which can be treacherous as hell? Or with unfriendly Indians, the worst risk of all?"

"Why, no experience, Pike. None! I and my son are from New York City, and all the soldiers and civilians with us hail from back East. We make no bones about it—that's why our troopers are well-armed, freed up for protection duty by non-hostile Shoshones hired for the dirty work." Here contempt spilled over into the officer's tone. "Not that the red niggers'll be enough help. I'm authorized, too, to hire white guides to supervise the Shoshones' feeble scouting efforts."

Ah, we come to the point, Pike thought. Aloud he said: "So, captain. That's why you want Skins's and my help. To act as guides and trouble-shooters."

"That's it!"

43

"No."

"No? You'll be well paid. Listen to the amount I'm offering . . ."

Pike turned his tone calm. "Captain, don't waste your breath. Dollars don't matter to me or Skins—not this time. You see, that's a big, beautiful hunk of country out there. I doubt anyplace else can hold a candle to it. But what Easterners want is hundreds— even thousands—of wagons crawling over the land. Bringing folks west and filling it up. Changing it."

The captain's smile was cool. "Of course civilization cries out to change it! There are farms to be plowed, mines to be dug, rivers to be dammed. Who'd want the wilderness to stay the same?"

"I do," declared Pike.

"So do I," McConnell concurred. "So, best not count on our help, Leland."

The captain's expression turned waspish. "I never expected . . ."

Fred Leland, standing behind his father, wore an uneasy expression. It was Dix, the scientist, who piped up. He spoke like a foreigner from Europe, which he was. "Gent-hull-men, please reconsider? In the name uff science?"

"Sorry, fellas," said Pike. "We've got us a hunting trip planned—have had it planned for quite a while. Moving out tomorrow at sunup. As for the later part of today, well we'd like to fit in a bit of drinking."

Lieutenant Meester gave an unpleasant snort. "Huh! Didn't I see you earlier with a woman? That gambling cheat's slut shill?"

Pike stepped up to tower over the squat man. "You against males getting together with females?"

McConnell tugged Pike's sleeve-fringe. "C'mon, let's get outa here. Why mess with army?"

"Maybe you're right. Still—"

"Ain't Melody waiting for you about now?"

Pike got the message. He turned on a moccasin-heel and shouldered out the tent flap.

Chapter 6

"So tomorrow's the day?" Pike asked the woman. They were back in his lodgings upstairs in the sleeping quarters.

"*You're* leaving Fort Laramie in the morning," she said. "Why not me? I need to get on with my life."

The big mountain man and Melody were slowly undressing each other, removing the garments piece by piece until both were completely and gloriously naked.

Tiny shudders passed through her body at the sight of this man. She felt his large organ stiffening against her lower belly.

Pike's mouth moved to her outthrust breasts, to find them smooth, pillow-soft and ready for his touch. Both nipples were taut, and he caressed them. With his other hand he combed her flourishing pubic patch.

Melody threw her head back and moaned, her palms locking Pike's muscled thighs and buttocks. Blood vessels in her temples began to pulse, as she felt his swollen cock lift even higher. The mountain man's lips roved down her throat, searched her arm-pit, found her breasts, but kept going. Across her ab-domen, downward to her sex cleft, and then his teeth nibbled and nibbled.

Meanwhile she toyed with his erection, tracing pat-terns on the large, mushroom-shaped head with her fingers. He became inflamed. Her lips ministered to his heavy testicles, and when their eyes met, hers were very bright.

His blood-engorged sex swayed before her en-chanted gaze like a cobra before a snake charmer. Reaching out, she tugged the elongated shaft with her fingers. Then she lowered her head, murmured to his purplish tip, "Pretty, big cock! You're all I've dreamed of all day. And now I'm going to make you mine, all mine!"

Melody's hand began to pump him eagerly, fast for a while, then even faster.

"Aah!" the mountain man gasped. "Oh, Jesus, that feels good!"

"Good? Then, the next I've got is going to feel just *terrific!*"

Melody clamped the hammerhead of rigidity be-tween her passionate lips, drawing in inches of him to fill her mouth from palate to throat. As she did, she moaned and groaned joyously. Pike felt his cock were drenched in a boiling whirlpool. Exploding tremors shot from his groin, to every nerve-end of his quaking frame. Not quite half his length had Melody sucked in, and aware of this, she continued to pump his stalk. As the woman assiduously flexed his love lance, she stroked his balls-purse as he cried out:

47

"Melody . . . Hot Damn! Ready or not, here I come! Aaar-aargghh!"

As the woman's head bobbed and her milky boobs swayed, her lips smacked as she sucked his rod. Melody's tongue flogged his fit-to-burst penile tip. Her free hand roaming to her own sexual parts, she found her love tab, which she fingered and skillfully massaged till pleasure flowed.

Melody shuddered with rapture as she felt Pike gush his load. It boiled over her tongue and down her gulping throat. When she'd sucked him dry, she gave him a worshipful look.

Desire was written on her face.

He'd seen that look before, and knew what to do.

"What a wonderful thing it is, Pike, your thing! Why, even now it hasn't grown the least bit soft."

She lifted her hips, and he entered her envelope. The wetness inside laved him with seething heat. With a sensuous gasp she took all of him that she could. She thought he'd scrape her backbone with his tremendous, throbbing pole.

"Oh, Pike, this is what I've needed! I'm flying to pieces. Oh, don't stop now . . . Oh, please don't stop!"

He almost lost her in the violent pumping, then rammed home again—and again. "Yes, oh, *yes!*" she exclaimed, the feeling in her loins peaking. Then her love channel spasmed, relaxed . . . spasmed, relaxed . . . spasmed, relaxed.

The man's and woman's pelvises slammed together. The couple's bodies were out of control— clutching, bucking and running sweat and other juices. With breathing ragged and heartbeats triphammering, they came tremendously, and at the same moment.

Melody's happy shriek was gusted to Pike's chest. "Oh, my God, Pike!" she wailed. "I'm filled. I've never been so filled."

He felt good too. Damned good.

They lay a long time together petting and nuzzling, but finally her eyelids grew heavy and she dropped off. As for Pike he lay facing the window, watching the sky in the west turn magenta-gold with blood-red streaks. He needed to make the rounds of the post, say some farewells to folks he knew, and also tell some things to McConnell. Also, the horses—both mounts and packers—needed a night-before-departure check.

Moving so as not to wake the woman, Pike rose from the bed. As quietly as a ghost he shrugged into his clothes, then slipped out the door and left her sleeping.

Darkness was fast settling down as Pike strode outside the walls toward the corral. And yet, when hailed by a voice, he immediately recognized its owner. "Standing Antelope." The mountain man greeted the Indian with pleasure. He accompanied his words with a hand sign that signified friendship. "You, here at Laramie? I'm glad to see you again, my brother."

The strapping, although middle-aged brave was smiling too. "This warrior's greeting go to you, He-Whose-Head-Touches-the-Sky. It's been many moons since last our paths crossed. My heart is glad this day."

"What brings you to the fort?" Pike asked, figuring the question a safe one. If the red man hadn't wanted palaver, he needn't have shown himself.

The Shoshone put his closed hand to the front of his quilled hide shirt. "Well, He-Whose-Head-Touches-the-Sky, Standing Antelope and some Shoshones from my village, we have gone to work for the Long Knives! Handling horses, scouting to see if enemies come near, showing the way through the mountains. Some of our women are along on the trip to cook and wash the Long Knives' clothes. I come from talking with the Long Knife chief, who tells me we leave soon for the big, sky-high mountains. Not war trip, this, but a trip for look-see."

"You're going with Leland and his soldiers on the mapping party? Well, you're mixed up with some real greenhorns, my brother."

"Earn plenty trade goods for the job—iron knives and hatchets, pretty cloth and blankets to keep our people warm next cold-wind moon. Carry 'em back to our village in the Western land."

Pike slapped the Indian's back. "The pay sounds good, and I wish you luck. But Standing Antelope, the bunch aims to head into Blackfeet territory."

"Shoshones not afraid of Blackfeet! We—"

Pike had heard Indians' boasting speeches before, and recalled that they could get lengthy. He was in a hurry now to get on with his rounds, and so spoke. "Hear my words, good friend. Take care of both yourself and your pretty daughter, Bright Cloud."

"How does my brother know Bright Cloud is with our group?"

"Well, I just saw her over your shoulder, over by the smithy, Standing Antelope, while you were saying how brave you were. Now the gal's vanished in the shadows."

"Standing Antelope will see her later in his lodge. Well, step carefully, He-Whose-Head-Touches-the-Sky."

"Step carefully, Standing Antelope."

Pike walked off shaking his head, glad he had nothing to do with Captain Leland, his mission or the people under his command—white folk or Shoshones. He had a hunch that trouble was brewing. When Pike had glimpsed Bright Cloud behind her father's back, she hadn't been alone—far from it.

Over by the smithy the maid in the doeskin dress had been in the arms of a man. First on the receiving end of an impassioned kiss, she'd next gone willingly with the man up an alley between two dark buildings.

Pike recognized the man because he'd met him just that day. And a West Point graduate—even a recent one—should have known enough not to get involved the way he was.

Wasn't Lieutenant Fred Leland aware of his pa's—the captain's—prejudice against red people? For the man kissing Bright Cloud had been young Fred Leland!

Pike moseyed on over to the corral, examined his and McConnell's horseflesh, and found the gray and the blaze-faced bay sound and ready. Then he retraced his steps back to the mess hall and taproom, wanting one last whiskey against the coming wilderness trek.

In the doorway to the noisy, smoke-filled hall, he was bumped by yet another old acquaintance. The man was in the far stages of drunkenness, had splashed crack-skull whiskey down the front of his buckskins, to mingle with traces of vomit. The man swung a jug from his trigger finger, and it sloshed. "O-outa m' way, mister! Outa th' way of ol' Muley Ballou, baddest-assed likker swiller and squaw-forker south 'o th' Yellerstone!"

"Be my guest in making it outside, Ballou." Pike had known the raunchy beaver-man and scout for years. He'd been in regular attendance at all the big trappers' rendezvous.

"P-pike? Jack Pike? Ol' Muley, he's drunk, sure, but damn it, let me tell ya 'bout m' windfall. Ballou, he's gonna take th' sojer-boys up inta th' mountains. Haw! Gonna be a guide, b'gawd. A guide!"

Then Ballou staggered out into the night, leaving Pike with the hunch that Leland's mission was jinxed indeed.

Chapter 7

Pike and McConnell, straddling the gray and the
bay and leading a couple of nondescript pack horses,
left Fort Laramie early in the morning, rode directly
into Laramie Range, then out the other side. Here the
great high plain sprawled toward the west, to where
the higher Rockies shouldered the sky. On up out of
the foothills the pair rode then, under a sky of flaw-
less blue. Virgin timber carpeted the slopes with
green, and the weather was glorious. The mountain
men's eyes told them it would stay that way for days
to come. Pike grinned at Skins with satisfaction, and
gigged his mount again.

The men's destination wasn't chosen yet; they only
knew they were off on a summer hunt. The plan was
to camp that night at Red-Stone Creek, and by morning make the big decision—to swing northward or
southward. To the south lay prime elk country, and
to the north the harsh, rugged range of the bighorn
sheep. Pike considered both species worthy prey,
leery of man and hard to approach. Still, it had been

years since he'd brought down a ram, and as he rode he found his mouth watering for mouthfuls gamy mutton.

"How far you reckon now till to Red-Stone?" McConnell called from his mount.

"Oh, we'll make it by nightfall. See that notch? Fix it in your mind real good."

He pointed ahead, at the saddle-dip between two peaks. And he found himself thinking of Melody Hooper. He scarcely missed her, not since he'd seen her leaving with the pack train bound for St. Louis. She'd grinned from her sidesaddle, waved and called, "I'm glad I'm going home, Pike! The West was a grand experience, and you were the best part. I'll never forget you, but it's back East where I'll be truly happy!"

She was a woman who'd made up her mind, and acted on it. Pike was satisfied with that. He just plain wasn't the kind to settle down. His first love was these mountains, as he again felt on this perfect day. The sun above welcomed him back to the high country. He partook of the grandeur, and was glad.

They followed the rugged trail, the setting sun, toward the stolid peaks that, purple and snow-capped, brushed the sky. The sky grew crimson-orange, and the men turned the horses down an incline. Rushing water could be heard. "Get ready, Skins. It's a helluva campsite."

There was a freshly rushing stream, plus grass for the animals. Within a half-hour the horses, hobbled, grazed contentedly. The mountain men's fishhooks had brought them two nice trout, and these were skewered on sticks over a small fire.

Beans and coffee completed the meal.

"I been thinking, Pike," McConnell said, chewing.

"Yeah?"

"About the hunt. I know you like elk meat, but . . ."

"Go on."

"I got this taste for mutton. Hell, those bighorns, I know they're hard to get to, but wouldn't it be worth it? I mean, yeah, buffalo hump makes delicious eating, but . . ."

Pike emptied coffee grounds from his tin cup. "Relax, Skins. We're of the same mind. I favor cutting north too, going after the sheep. Pretty country up that way. Be good to see it again."

Later, bedded down, they lay looking at the sky. The air was so clear, the stars exploded across the firmament, their beaconing light sheened the trees and rock faces silver. "Y'know . . ."

"Yeah, Skins?"

"This is a pretty spot. These mountains hold a lot of 'em—pretty spots. I've been thinking about those soldier boys. Is that map-making thing gonna raise a settlers' boom?"

Pike studied on the question. Then said, "However things turn out, the end's a good many years off. Give conditions back East time to go from bad to worse. There, the rich control things like crop prices, rents. Taxes are high. That's why poor folks want to see the West opened."

"Wanting free land?"

"Or minerals, or just good wages. Trapping too. A trapper can take eight or ten beaver a day. With what plews are selling for, that's two weeks' wages in a place like Louisville."

"True," McConnell muttered drowsily. "True."

Then the last thing before he dozed, "Wonder how things are in Leland's camp about now."

The soldiers, civilians and Shoshones had made camp early, but as usual, had wasted time. It was an hour after dark before supper was dished up, and then it was salt pork and hardtack. The marksmen, poor shots, had failed to bag enough game. The placement of the encampment wasn't ideal, but there was a spring, though a sluggish one. A recent flash flood had soaked the ground wood and the fires smoked, laying down a sooty pall.

Lieutenant Frederic Leland sat on a deadfall and forked down the fatty, tasteless mess. Through the walls of his father's tent he could see the silhouette—the captain was seated at his table. Everyone in the party knew the commanding officer's menu was fresh quail. Standing Antelope had brought in two birds, and they'd quickly been "requisitioned."

Fred tossed the dregs of his coffee, if one could call it coffee. Next he glanced at Meester, who was technically his superior. Meester, the "leader of men," enjoyed pulling rank on Fred, the expedition's regular-army naturalist. To Meester, Fred's notebooks on flora and fauna were a joke.

To Fred, they were more important than anything. Well, almost anything . . .

Bright Cloud strolled by, the raven braids that framed her copper-hued features falling down the front of her dress. The doeskin garment was a work of art, being beaded with colorful, complex designs. But the dress was eclipsed by the woman, who was graceful as well as young, pretty of smile and enchanting of form.

As she went into the forest, she didn't twitch her hips. She didn't need to, Fred Leland got up and followed. Although he walked on fir needles and humus, he still made noise.

That's how she knew he'd arrived at the glade.

Her father, Standing Antelope, was on the other side of the camp with the other Indians, so the woman felt safe. When Fred came to her, she ran into his arms. Fred brushed her lips, and she responded with fire!

They sank on bed-soft duff, her fringed dress hiked high. She was a naked vision. Feeble moonlight turned her copper skin silver. His lips closed on her eager mouth, and she opened it wide, engulfing his tongue. Exquisite tremors shook her slim frame, as through the cloth of his uniform she felt his manhood stiffen. Quickly she worked at his buttons, opening his pants to set free the prisoner. His lance-haft largeness stood up straight. The hairy sack beneath looked like a stuffed medicine pouch.

She felt him with an engaging touch. He found her small, pear-shaped breasts, each one of which promised a delicious feast. Soot-gray areolas surrounded her nipples, which went pebble-hard at his worshipful touch.

Fred Leland bent low and sucked, and the nipple swelled to his slippery tongue. His hand roamed below the dress, to delve into her lava-hot love channel.

The passion in his loins building, the good-looking officer reared up to enter Bright Cloud. As she looked up at him, her dark, liquid eyes swam. Combing the few black strands of hair at her portal with his phallus tip, he was delighted at the flow of scented nectar.

His swaying maleness arrowed toward its goal, and the woman acted as guide, positioning it. As he plunged past her portal, her shapely legs trembled. She moaned aloud, eager for what he offered.

Kindling his own delight and his dark-eyed partner's, the lieutenant drove his flagpole at her satin folds. "Ah!" she cried. "Ah! Aaiiee! Oh, Fred, . . . Oh, Fred . . ."

Sounds like pounding surf assaulted Fred's ears, and in the young officer's remembrance appeared Long Island, the wave-battered sand spit below his family's mansion. How ironic that that life seemed eons in the past! Fred felt his life from now on was in the arms of this Indian girl.

His jetting syrup lavishly drenched her channel, as together they swam the wave-crest of release. Then down, down they cascaded, embracing. Oblivious to all, the man flopped slack atop her.

She in turn hugged him with all her strength, her handsome, beloved white man.

* * *

Orlo Brubaker scratched what itching whip scars he could reach beneath his uniform blouse, muttering under his breath a low "Goddamn." As yet the welts and cuts left by Sergeant O'Dell's whip had only half-healed. Military discipline—in the form of corporal punishment administered while away from an army fort—had been rough, but even more hateful had been Orlo's mental state.

Every day now the half-breed trooper seethed, angry over the loss of the money he'd expected from the sale of stolen guns.

He was filled with rage even now, tramping from camp into the woods in order to relieve his bladder. Directing his stream at a tree trunk, he scowled and scanned his dark surroundings. Although he saw nothing, he could hear something.

A liquid-sounding *slap-slap*.

Christ! Can't be the sound of fucking. Who's there to fuck?

Sneaking through wild mulberry shrubs, he came upon the lovers' feast of flesh, now in its cool-down phase. He could scarcely see in the deep shadows, but a musical voice tittered out a laugh, fixing the couple's location. And then a man's voice said: "There, there, Bright Cloud. I've fixed your dress. Your father'll never know."

It was a voice Orlo had heard barking orders. Lieutenant Leland? It was surely he. Orlo Brubaker hated authority, and he hated the Lelands, father and son. And now, he'd caught the son with his pants down, literally!

And with the pretty, hot-assed squaw!

"Orlo Brubaker, here's luck for you, b'gawd!"

He still dreamed of making off with government muskets. Only now, he thought, to hell with selling to whites, as Milt had wanted. Better to let the "thunder sticks" go to the Blackfeet, the tribe of Orlo's mother among whom he'd been raised. Orlo recalled Angry Bear, the leader of his clan. The chief, although savage, knew a good thing. The tribesmen had nuggets to trade, and furs, and they'd pay almost anything to achieve White Eyes' firepower.

Orlo skulked back toward the encampment, his mind alive.

How to most profitably commit blackmail?

The half-breed would study on it.

Chapter 8

"We know where the bighorn sheep'll be taking themselves this season, don't we?" Skins observed to Pike.

"The real high country."

"Yeah, the real high country."

"A happy hunting ground up there."

With that Pike had to agree also. They were riding their geldings side-by-side on another fine day, the dome of sky blue overhead, with golden eagles coasting on high. The territory they crossed was rarely traveled, consisting of spectacular divides and towering crags, down from which dropped cliffs into thousand-feet-deep gorges.

Most of the spruce and cedar forests were interspersed with aspens. Whenever they crossed creeks the rushing waters were clear and sparkling. The view on all sides was nothing short of breathtaking.

"Y'know, Skins, those bighorn rams, they're the hardest critters of all to bag. Got 'em the sharpest eyes, keep to the roughest, highest ground."

"That's why we're going after 'em this trip, Jack. For the challenge. Look, this new rifle I got, it's a Hawken like yours. I got to try it out."

"You *have* tried it out."

"Oh, shit, yes! On antelope and deer!"

"Like to put a small bet on this sheep hunt? As to who turns out to be the best marksman?"

McConnell rode in silence for a while, thinking. Then, "You said a small bet. How small?"

"Well-l-l, something like next season's first week of taken beaver plews?"

Skins winced. "That bet's far from small. In fact, it's steep."

"I thought you called yourself a fair shot."

"But those sheep are leery. The rifle range could run up as far as two-hundred yards, across gorges with terrific wind-drifts. Where the altitude's so high a shooter's eyes get misted."

Pike, with a grin, went, "Cluck, cluck, cluck."

"You calling me chicken?"

"If the moccasin fits . . ."

McConnell slapped his cantle hard, and the rifle strapped to his shoulder slipped. He caught the weapon before it started to fall, and grumbled, "All right, Jack, I'll take your action! But next season's first week's catch? What do you say to makin' the bet the first *two* weeks' catch?"

"Done!"

"Shake on it?"

"Shake!"

The horses seemed friskier after that, perhaps sensing the good spirits in their riders. Pike was eager indeed, but not just because of the bet.

There *was* something about the challenge of the huntsman's sport. Plus he'd pumped up his appetite for prime mountain mutton. If the weather held, the week to come looked like a damned pleasant one.

If the weather held, and the Blackfeet kept minding their own business!

They rode into the high country where the chill winds swept along ceaselessly. The snowcapped Bitterroots towered on all sides and the streams plunged down steep channels, surging as they made their way to distant seas. Pike and McConnell passed alpine meadows ringed with aspen, and on going higher, came to thick stands of pine. The forests teemed with elk, deer and all kinds of smaller game. But the mountain men's goal this time was sheep, and they'd be sticking to that.

After two more days of climbing, the magnificent peaks were snow-streaked. The trail the mountain men took was rugged and broken, in places covered with shattered rock and washed-down dirt. Sometimes the horses walked a narrow ledge, swaying dangerously over a sheer drop-off. "At least we haven't seen any Indian sign," McConnell joked once.

Pike laughed. "Right. No Indian sign."

They crossed the Great Divide, turned from the main trail down into a pristine valley. In the valley's center was a jewel-blue lake. Reigning in on an outcropping, Pike called, "Good place for a camp. Good water and grass. Signs of big game."

"And no signs of redskins."

"You got Indians on the brain?"

"Want to know what I've got on the brain? Mountain sheep!" McConnell's horse tossed its head, and the rider reached down to pat its withers. But his hand froze in the motion.

"Jack! Look up yonder slope!"

Pike used his hand to shade his eyes and looked. He saw a ram of rather small size, plus a number of ewes and some lambs that gamboled. The hillside where they grazed was a considerable distance. Disappointment crept into McConnell's voice.

"Well, the horns on that ram are a mite spindly."

"Let's make camp and take our guns out in the morning."

"Well, if you say so, Jack."

"Relax, Skins. You'll get your shot at a big fella."

Duck Wing, a big strapping brave, gestured to his companion Heavy Mink. The track of Wapiti, the bull elk, was cut deeply in the turf. The young Indian hunters nocked arrows to their bows, slid down the ridge behind which they'd left their ponies tied.

Such was the wisdom of the pair's tribe, the mighty Blackfeet people: go on foot after the powerfully antlered ones. Elks, male and female both, were wary animals, but the full-grown herd leaders were the real survivors, so honed by instinct were their senses.

This hunt far from their band's village hadn't turned

out successful for the two young men. They'd hoped to return home bearing meat and trophies. But now the key to turning their luck around appeared to be at hand. All it would take was to bring down a great bull elk, one with an especially fine hide and impressive antler rack.

A huge knob of boulder speared from the side of a hill, and around it the stealthy red men made their way. They passed through a sparse pine grove, keeping their eyes on the ground more than the surrounding mountains. Three horse–lengths ahead they saw the edge of a glade. Elks liked to feed in glades.

True, venturing into a glade could spell trouble should any white men be near. Like all Blackfeet, Duck Wing and Heavy Mink hated the White Eyes. But just now they gave warlike notions short shrift. There were no white men they knew of in the vicinity, and they were onto something else.

Through the trees they heard the clatter of hooves on rocky ground—and a whistle-like bugling. They hurried forward on silent moccasins, expecting to find elk, yet as always, prepared for the unexpected.

"Look, my brother. Over there!"

Duck Wing pointed, and glided forward. His friend was at his heels, his mouth a tightly pressed slit. Two great elk bulls were engaged in battle, presumably for possession of a herd of cows that were nowhere in sight.

"My brother, I see many knife handles in those horns."

"And the hides, they're fine ones for a special purpose I have in mind," Heavy Mink went on to explain. "Medicine shirts! The kind that magically protects the wearer against the White Eyes' thunder sticks."

So far the elks' fight had been a hard one. The ground was trampled over almost an acre. The two bulls appeared evenly matched, being of nearly the same size, with one's antlers only two points shy of the other's.

Duck Wing signaled his partner to take the bull with the lighter-colored hair. He'd take the darker one, by sneaking close, driving a flint-tipped arrow into that well-muscled neck.

Again the elks bugled, pawed the earth a few times and charged. Their heads lowered to bring the antlers into play. Their rumps surged and their legs pumped, and they ran directly at each other full tilt. When the animals collided head-on, antlers interlocked with a loud, jolting *thwack*.

Both men drew their bowstrings to their copper cheeks. But before they could let fly, a gunshot echoed down the mountainside.

Both elks bolted, and were gone in a flash. The Indians stood flat-footed, letting their bowstrings go slack. Then outrage tinged their features, anger lit their black eyes.

Duck Wing hissed, "A White Eyes, maybe more than one. Carrying thunder sticks. Up there."

Heavy Mink stroked a rope-like hair braid. "On the heights, where live *Mata-shu*, the mountain sheep!"

"My brother, what do you say? Shall we go hunting for scalps this day?"

"You know the answer to that." The brave's hand went to the tomahawk at his waist. "Blackfeet warriors live to gain the honor of killing enemies. Any place, any time! And the scalps of those White Eyes up there? My brother, they'll hang from our belts before Father Sun leaves Mother Sky."

Chapter 9

The party of blue-coats, with their hired Shoshones keeping pace, rode the southerly trail that led to Wild Horse Gap, proposed by some a possible short route over the Divide. Only time and accurate measurements would tell. Captain Leland rode with Chief Scout Muley Ballou at the head of the winding column of mounted men.

"Ballou," the commandant was saying, "I want to push the men harder, make better time."

The buckskinned graybeard wagged his head, and puckered his walnut-brown, seamed face. "Don't reckon that'll work out, cap'n. Not and be wise, it can't."

The white scout turned in the saddle, glanced over his shoulder at the men following along the trail behind. The day was uncomfortably warm, and only Captain Leland wore his insignia-studded wool overjacket. The troops and junior officers rode in shirts unbuttoned at the collars and with sleeves rolled up. Of course, they all wore regulation light-blue trousers, stuffed into the tops of knee-cut Jefferson boots.

"What do you mean, scout, 'not and be wise'?"

Under bushy brows, Ballou's bloodshot eyes danced. "Weel, cap'n, for one thing, the horses. Play *them* out and we'll all be in a bad fix. That bein' the case, we can't afford to skip stops for waterin' and restin' the stock. So the onliest way to make up time, it'd be ridin' later on into evening. But see, in Injun country, you make camp after dark, it's askin' for trouble. There's pitchin' of the half-pups, buildin' of fires, eatin'—all with the men busy with chores, and weapons laid by. Why, we'd be sittin' ducks."

"I see." Maynard Leland's look was cold. "Well, maybe we'll keep on as we've been doing. That's all for now, Ballou."

Taking the hint, the buckskinned man spurred his mount out ahead of the column. He'd make a pretense of scouting the next bend. Actually, he'd dismount, relieve his bladder, and give his tailbone what he considered a well-earned rest.

The mountains the party rode through rose tall and proud, cutting off much of the sky. The slopes rolling away were covered with timber stands green as baize poker tables. Melchior Dix rode with his notebook open on his thigh, logging the contours of the imposing land. He saw the terrain as a map in his brain, a great, wide, open country stretching hundreds and hundreds of miles in all directions.

The old man, swaying tirelessly in the saddle, was

continually making crude maps on paper, marking down all the major landmarks. Peaks and gorges, watercourses and divides—all that came to view got sketched in accurately. Often Dix called a halt, hauled out his barometer, took a measurement of altitude. But what seemed most important to the scientist were the grade angles up and over notches.

He was always seeking the ultimate low pass, one that could easily be negotiated by wagons. After all, wasn't that the purpose of the trip? To make maps that would lead settlers to, and over, the Rockies so the great American West could grow and go on growing?

Fred Leland sat on the plodding horse with its burned "USA" brand on the rump, jolting on his butt-busting McClellan saddle, his mind wandering from his duties. As an expedition naturalist he was assigned to keep notes of plants and wild animals he caught sight of, as well as weather conditions and nature of the soil. The first weeks after leaving Laramie he'd worked eagerly, since he was trained for the work and believed in its value.

But now he found it very hard to concentrate.

Ever since rising this morning at the crack of dawn, his mind had been harder than ever to keep off Bright Cloud.

The Shoshone beauty was an endless source of fascination for the young officer from New York. Each time he'd lain with her it had been a new experience, so different from relations with girls he'd known back East.

Bright Cloud sent his desire rocketing through the skies, and Fred had wondered why, until he'd managed to pinpoint the reasons. There was certainly the young woman's beauty, from classic facial features to the thick, raven hair. But neither was there coyness or pretension in her makeup.

The sex act, for Bright Cloud, was completely natural. As natural for the young woman as for a healthy, uninhibited forest creature.

Fred's thoughts were interrupted when Orlo Brubaker gigged his horse alongside. The officer hated the sight of the man who'd been caught stealing guns, especially now, since his face wore a cunning cast.

Now Orlo grunted: "Beg pardon, leftenant. With your permission, sir?"

Fred winced at the man's smirk. The fellow stank of horses, manure, dust. "Permission not granted, private. Fall back in line!"

"But it's important. About somethin' I know regardin' you, leftenant."

"Take your place in the column. That's an order."

"But . . ."

The lieutenant's nose went up, and his lip curled. "You *do* know about orders, private? And the risk you take, not following 'em?"

Orlo Brubaker cringed. The scarred skin of his back crawled. He reined his remount horse into line, prepared to eat dust.

"Goddamned shavetail," he cursed. Then, to himself, Gonna make it hard, ain't you? The best scheme

I've thunk up since the gun-thievin' deal went bust? Well, maybe tonight I'll get to you yet, leftenant, after camp's pitched. He hated both Lelands now, as well as Sergeant Patrick O'Dell and the whole damned United States Army.

He was looking forward to putting guns in the hands of Blackfeet warriors.

"The better to blow you bastards outa your saddles," he snarled. "And sojers' topknots sure do look fine hangin' bloody in the villages, from high ol' lodge-pole ends."

Chapter 10

"Damn it, Jack!" Skins McConnell howled. "Missed him! Had him right in my sights and missed the ram!"

"There'll be other rams," Pike consoled.

"This one was big, Jack. Mighty big. And he bolted when I fired. You never got to take your own shot."

Pike tugged down his hatbrim, checked the priming on his Hawken after the brief exciting time. "Skins, best get your gun reloaded for another stalk. How's the old saying go? No use crying over spilled milk."

They'd risen before sunup, breakfasted on jerky and biscuits, washed down with coffee strong enough to float a horseshoe. Saddling up the gray and the bay geldings and swinging aboard, they started for the mountainside opposite, where scattered on the open slopes some mountain sheep could be seen.

"Now, the wild woolies," Pike told his pard, "they'll keep their distance."

"I know it," McConnell said.

"Especially those old, savvy rams."

"Oh, *don't* I know it! Say Jack, you want to flap your jaws or hunt?"

"What do you think?"

"Hunt."

"Remember the bet we made a while back, Jack?"

"I remember it."

"I just wanted to make sure."

"Hey, Skins? You want to go hunting this morning, or just jog along flapping your jaws?"

The mountain men crossed the rock-strewn flats on horseback, but on reaching a broad, tawny rock face they picketed the animals and stood staring up at where they'd need to go on their own legs. After two-hundred or so yards of easy going, they were going to have to clamber up steep gullies and the remains of landslides, among fast-flowing freshets and over slippery rocks.

"Oughtn't we try and travel light?" Skins asked.

"Light, how do you mean?"

"Well, we'll need our rifles, and of course powder horns and shot pouches, but what about these Kentucky pistols? They're heavy pieces, and almost useless in a hunt."

"Be handy, though, if we get jumped by enemies."

"What enemies? We're in the heart of—if you'll pardon the expression—virgin wilderness. Jack, you seen any people, any *sign* of people, white or red, for a hundred miles?"

"No."

"So we leave the Kentucky pistols on the horses' saddles. The saved weight'll make for an easier climb."

"I'll go along with you this time, Skins. But don't ask me to shed my tomahawk or my Green River–style skinning knife."

"Tomahawks and knives, they're good for butchering kills. I aim to fetch back to camp every pound of meat we can."

So they set off up-slope, carrying their rifles primed and ready. At the first almost-vertical stretch of climbing, the mountain men's legs began to tighten up and ache. As they went higher and higher, they found their ears popping. Once, twice, three times the hunters skirted groups of ewes and lambs, realizing that to spook them would spook the wily old sire, their prey.

"Glad we saved ourselves packing those Kentucky pistols?"

"It's a hell of a climb, Skins. Maybe you were right, trading saved weight against an extra bit of protection."

At last they came to timberline, dominated by grim-looking and gray granite escarpments. Up here the keening of the wind was a constant, the pinyon trees were all "flagged," the branches growing only on the side away from the prevailing wind.

A movement up ahead caught Pike's sharp eye, and he hissed, "There, Skins . . . Yonder!" On a cliff-top a half-mile off stood a bighorn ram of truly noble proportions. It was muscular and its cape was thickly haired. It also sported a whopping pair of horns.

"Now there's a hide for keeping a fella warm," said Skins.

"Plus meat for eating, and horns for making folks' eyes pop back at the trading post."

"*And* a dandy target for our shooting match," McConnell added.

"Ah, the shooting match. How could I forget?"

"Two weeks' trapping pelts come next season. I'm looking forward to collecting."

Skins checked the priming on his rifle. "Well, what the hell we waiting for, Jack? Shall we stir our stumps, take us on up there into range?"

Keeping themselves concealed in draws and rock cuts, they began their stalk. Although the hard ground was covered with loose stones, the feet of the mountain men dislodged but few. Skill in moving silently was one trait of a real mountain man.

At last they gained a rock ledge where they had the view they wanted.

Skins elbowed Pike without speaking. The least noise now could frighten the big sheep.

It was clear to Pike that the ram sported enormous horns, with a thirty-six-inch curl to them at least. The tips were cracked and marred, the result of battles over years of mating seasons. The only problem for the shooters now was distance. The critter was at least a hundred-and-fifty yards off, and the breeze was stiff.

Pike pointed at McConnell, signaling who should take the shot. Then the bigger mountain man removed his hat to let his hair be teased by the air. Skins cocked his Hawken and pointed it, then glanced at Pike's blowing hair, making a shrewd estimate of wind drift.

McConnell triggered.

The lead ball carried low, slamming a rock face.

The big sheep bolted off the ridge with a mighty leap, sped bounding down the slope. Inside of two seconds the magnificent animal was out of view.

"Damn it, Jack, missed him! Had him right in my sights and missed the ram!"

The only thing left was to try another stalk. Pike told McConnell so, and McConnell agreed. So they threaded their way back down the rock-bound crevice they'd come up, moccasin soles sliding on sharp talus shards, taking handholds where they could, even protruding rock points that broke off when grabbed.

The mountain men rapidly descended more than five-hundred feet, after which the grade leveled off, and brittle shrubbery became available to grab. Then Pike led the way onto an unfamiliar trail, along a rocky ridge that shortly became a granite ledge with a hundred-foot drop-off.

"Holy smoke," blurted McConnell. "I don't remember coming up this way."

"Look at it as a short-cut, friend," Pike said. "See, the ledge takes us to that tree-grown level stretch, and once through the trees we're almost where the big ram disappeared. It's our best chance of locating him again."

"Our best chance?"

"Our best. And don't you want more contest shots? Give yourself a chance to score, me to miss, make a fool of myself?"

Skins grinned. "Yeah, I *would* like to see you left holding the bag."

But at that very moment Pike, always alert to movement, saw an Indian coming at them through the trees. By the look of his breechclout and headband, the lone brave was a Blackfoot. Worse, he'd daubed his face and chest with clay in a display of improvised war paint.

Apparently the brave had been walking, bow in hand. Now he broke into a run at the white men, his voice lifted in a war whoop.

The mountain men dropped to their knees, thumbed the hammers of their rifles back, drew beads on the Indian. "A Blackfoot, and he's on the prod! I'll shoot first, Skins! Hold your fire. There maybe are more of 'em about."

"Right, Jack!"

But as it turned out, neither mountain man got to draw a bead.

From a steepling boulder just behind them another redskin dropped. Duck Wing, springing his trap, landed on the ledge close to the mountain men, arms outstretched to knock their rifles from their hands. "Ha-ya-yeeeh!" he yelled, exulting.

The hammer of Pike's Hawken detonated the charge with a loud *boom*. The lead ball tore a fist-size chunk of wood from an aspen near Heavy Mink.

Heavy Mink's arrow zipped by McConnell's ear, struck the boulder face and glanced away.

Now the two brawny young warriors stood in the trail, confronting the mountain men. They'd dropped their bows and now brandished tomahawks.

Pike and McConnell, their rifles useless, drew their own tomahawks from their belt sheaths.

Pike grinned at McConnell, and McConnell grinned at Pike. Both felt the exhilaration that preceded a good fight. ''So we've got no guns this time. Let's give 'em hell anyway, Skins!''

''Here we go. Hang on to your topknot, pard!''

Chapter 11

It was a script the mountain men had played to before, a fight to the death against bloodthirsty Indian foes. Only this time Pike and McConnell were without guns. Each hefted a weighty tomahawk in his big hand, knowing the awful damage the weapons were capable of. But both the Blackfeet warriors were armed with tomahawks too. . . .

Suddenly the taller Indian, Duck Wing, let out an ear-splitting war whoop and charged.

Pike moved quickly for a man so big, swiftly closing the distance between him and the Indians. As he and Duck Wing came together, the redskin's tomahawk glinted in the cold, clear sunlight. He launched a mighty chop, nearly taking Pike's head off. To avoid the blow, Pike threw himself on his back and kicked out, using both feet. The kick failed to dislodge the tomahawk from the Blackfoot's grasp.

The Blackfoot, still gripping his weapon, loomed over the white man for the kill. Pike twisted aside as the redskin lunged, then rolled to his feet and lashed out with his own hatchet.

The weapons clashed and rang like dinner bells, steel meeting steel. Seeing his vicious sweeps parried, the mountain man kicked out again, this time aiming for the Blackfoot's kneecap. The warrior was a skilled fighter too, agile and sure-footed. He stepped aside, slammed his own foot into Pike's thigh. He'd tried for the groin, but Pike, anticipating the move, avoided it.

McConnell had closed with an enemy too, and Heavy Mink, although a squat man, was a dangerous foe. He scythed with his tomahawk like a crazed lumberjack, and only Skins's own skill enabled him to hold ground.

Eyes flashing hate, Heavy Mink chopped and chopped, but McConnell brought up his own weapon, deflecting every swing. Still, the mountain man's footwork was hasty and his shin sideswiped a rock. He felt himself toppling. He hit the flinty trail elbow-first and a sharp bolt of pain surged down his forearm to his fingertips!

A sensation of numbness soon replaced the pain. The tomahawk dropped from McConnell's fingers. The Blackfoot circled as the mountain man regained his feet, his own tomahawk raised and ready. The mountain man ran at his opponent and the two grappled. McConnell held the red man's weapon away with his left hand, but Heavy Mink wrapped an arm around Skins's neck. McConnell backpedaled into the pull, and the Indian went off balance. Both foes fell,

McConnell barehanded and desperate, Heavy Mink armed and dangerous as hell!

Pike, too, seemed to have his hands full. He and his opponent exchanged a flurry of tomahawk chops, most of them fended off. Then a blow of Duck Wing's grazed Pike's skull, tearing out a clump of hair, starting a flow of blood. But the mountain man tornadoed with energy, wading in again, each whistling swing forceful.

Again Pike used his foot, powering his heel into the Indian's solar plexus. The Blackfoot halted as though mule-kicked, staggered back. Pike forced Duck Wing back . . . back . . .

Pike only wished he were free to help his partner. Through low-hanging boughs of a silver spruce he could see Skins battling. McConnell and his adversary rolled on the ground, the Blackfoot's tomahawk missing blows, Skins hanging on desperately.

His right arm almost useless, McConnell gave his body a twist, breaking the Indian's hold. Skins drove his head into the warrior's nose, and heard the rending of cartilage. Hot blood gushed from coppery nostrils, showering both men. The Indian roared with pain and anger and once more tried a death blow.

McConnell shot out his feet and pushed the Blackfoot off, then jumped up, only to see the Blackfoot regain his footing as well.

Skins swallowed a curse at the damage done to his

arm—he needed all his breath for fighting. The Blackfoot came at him and McConnell saw his hatchet flash. He dodged. The defensive move emboldened the warrior and he again charged, swinging viciously.

Pike's enemy had further retreated, and now both combatants faced each other on the narrow ledge. To the mountain man's left reared the towering stone wall, and on his right the sheer precipice dropped off five hundred feet, at least. The muscular, sweating Blackfoot darted close, then feinted. Pike launched an overhand blow that missed the Indian and hammered rock.

Pike's tomahawk slipped and spiraled into the abyss.

He jerked his Green River knife from his belt, but was backed to the wall.

McConnell dropped to a crouch in order to avoid an ax-swipe. Heavy Mink's arcing blow swept off Skins's hat, and the brave's momentum drove him into the mountain man. As they collided McConnell straightened, powering with his leg muscles to flip the Blackfoot. As the warrior bit the dust, Skins aimed a kick that took the Blackfoot in the head. The Indian sidelonged, but still gripped his tomahawk.

McConnell threw a roundhouse left to the painted chin.

* * *

Duck Wing slashed out, and Pike sucked in his gut, feeling the blade of the hatchet snag his buckskins' front. There was not an inch of room for Pike to step back. And behind the Blackfoot's was the bottomless drop-off. Here stood two bold fighters in their prime, each one's skills standing between him and death. Pike knew the Indian, as did he, honored courage more than life.

The white man hissed, "Blackfoot, you're a worthy foe. You've got a tomahawk, where I've only got my trusty Green River. But you're far from having this fight won. No, by thunder!"

The Blackfoot grunted something in his own language. A threat? A curse?

Then he came at Pike again, with a wild scream.

Pike wielded his razor-sharp blade and the Indian backed up fast, crow-hopping. Pike brought his point up, trying for the belly, but the Blackfoot danced aside, countering with his own tomahawk slash. But Pike's free hand vised the Blackfoot's wrist, and the two men went down again. Locked together, they rolled and rolled, coming to rest with Pike's shoulderblades hanging over the cliff's edge.

Heavy Mink's head was jolted by McConnell's punch, and the weapon flew from his hand. McConnell kicked it away, scooped it up with his good left hand. The Blackfoot dived for him, and he met the dive with a mighty upward chop.

The blade of the tomahawk landed with a meaty *thunk*. Heavy Mink stopped, amazement on his painted face. Looking down, he saw a half–pound of steel buried in his chest, spirals of lung tissue leaking past crushed bone, his whole front washed by a gouting blood-fountain.

The Blackfoot's eyes rolled back as he sank. He hit the ground face-first, but was dead by then.

Pike and Duck Wing squirmed and wrestled, locked chest-to-chest, the smell of each man in the other's nostrils. Pike's straining muscles stretched to the breaking point. His knife was poised above the Indian, where his wrist was locked. But he knew that the point was slowly descending, and Duck Wing knew it too!

With a last, frantic twist, the Indian tried to turn the tables. Instead, the mountain man's Green River drove in just below his short ribs. It angled upward, the blade slashing and mauling flesh. Duck Wing's chest cavity filled with blood, which bubbled up and spewed from his screaming mouth.

The corpse collapsed in Pike's arms. Gore smeared Pike's beard as he pushed away from the Blackfoot.

He stood, shoving back his sandy hair. He saw McConnell staggering toward him. "Well, Skins?"

"Well, Jack, we're alive."

"Still."

"Sure feels good. That cut on your head?"

"Hardly hurts. That dangling arm of yours?"

"The feeling's coming back. Which reminds me, are there more Blackfeet close by?"

"It's something to think on."

"To hell with the hunting trip. I don't hanker to take on a whole war party."

The men retrieved their rifles, and standing over the grisly corpses of the Blackfeet, carefully reloaded and primed the weapons. When he was finished, Pike picked up Duck Wing's tomahawk, wiped off a smear of the Indian's blood, then stuffed the weapon under his belt.

"Oh, by the way," Pike said. "About that contest . . ."

"What contest?" McConnell's face was open, innocent-looking.

Pike grinned.

No disturbance broke the wilderness calm.

Chapter 12

Melchior Dix and Lieutenant Fred Leland were sitting up late at night, atop a mounding outcrop that overlooked the camp. The cook fires had burned down to heaps of glowing coals, and the scattered half-pup tents of the men, who by now were sleeping, were given a ghostly sheen by the silver moonlight. The night was little different from every clear night since the expedition had started from Fort Laramie.

The head scientist had star sightings to make.

Dix lifted his sextant and pointed it at the sky. The telescope part of the instrument was glued to his eye, as he scanned about until he focused the North Star. Fred sat at the scientist's side, an open logbook in his lap, as well as a high-quality chronometer.

"Ready . . . mark it down," said Dix.

Being well past midnight, all was still but for the occasional howling of a distant wolf. All around the camp the mountains seemed to glower, their vast shapes menacing in darkness. Private Crank was on a hillside keeping watch on the remuda, but Fred didn't know who the camp sentry was at the moment, only that a short time earlier the guard had been changed. The young officer, scribbling a notation, squinted in the feeble candlelight. Dix was engaged in another sighting, this time using a star in a different part of the sky.

"Iss the fifth clear night in a row. Goot," said Dix, his accent rough as usual.

"Good for the logbook, maybe." Fred rubbed his eyes. "Staying up like this, night after night, really robs us of our rest."

The scientist's voice took on an aggrieved tone. "Do not forget, Frederic, this iss the reason for the expedition. Each night we're able, we calculate our exact position. Our map will be based on truly scientific information, for once."

He painstakingly corrected his lens adjustment. He was ready to take another crucial reading. "Now, record it. There, that iss all for tonight. Will you be going to your tent now, get the sleep you say you are needing?"

Dix busied himself replacing the sextant in its carrying case. "In a few minutes, Melchior. You go ahead down to the tents." Fred stood up and walked briskly to and fro, flexing his arms to shake loose cramps gained from sitting. But almost immediately, he bumped into a shadowy form.

"Sentry? What's up?"

"Maybe the jig's up, leftenant." Fred recognized a voice he didn't care to hear, now, or at any time. The voice of Orlo Brubaker.

"You're out of order, private! Your insolent."

"Hold on, leftenant. Best you pay attention. Y'see, I been spyin' on you and the purty squaw. Ah, I see *that* got your attention. What I got to say's this, if you wanta keep fuckin' her, you're gonna have pay me."

Fred was now on his feet. Dix was downslope, out of earshot. Leland eyed the sentry coldly. "Is this blackmail? You think I'd pay you to keep quiet about me and Bright Cloud?"

"I don't reckon your pa knows 'bout you and the squaw. One thing sure, he hates red niggers. Sure, you love the brown gal, but your pa, he'll want to cut her off from you. And bein' in command, he can send Standing Antelope away, order the chief to take his daughter with him." The scruffy soldier chuckled. "Next thing you know, old Leland'll be commandin' you to marry some Eastern cunt. One with pancake tits and icewater in her veins."

In the darkness, Brubaker's voice rasped on. "For keepin' mum, leftenant, here's what I'm asking. A hundred dollars in crisp greenbacks tonight, and the next payment, due in a few weeks."

Fred, with effort, kept his clenched fists at his sides. "You're scum, Brubaker. Get away from me!"

"But . . ."

"Get away, or I'll knock you down!"

To add emphasis, Leland took a roundhouse swing at the soldier, fanned air.

"Oh, I'll go, leftenant, I'll go! But in the mornin' I'll be palaverin' with the cap'n."

Brubaker vanished into shadows. Fred Leland kicked a rock and swore, "Son of a bitch!"

It wasn't that he feared the trooper, or whatever

slurs he might spread. Right now, Fred didn't even fear his father. Instead, the young man was experiencing a need for Bright Cloud's body. Here, on the mountainous hillside. Now, at an hour well past midnight.

And with the woman this much in his thoughts, a gigantic erection was building under cover of his trouser front.

A shooting star went blazing overhead. Fred planted his rump on a flat rock and sat looking at the ground, his teeth grinding with anger and frustration.

Wait! he suddenly thought. *Maybe I don't need to lose Bright Cloud on account of Brubaker!*

And now, as he looked up at the spangled sky, his mind was forming a plan.

Chapter 13

Sunrise made a fan of orange and gold across the peaks to the east that seemed to roof the world. Captain Maynard Leland stepped out of his tent intending to greet the glorious Rocky Mountain morning.

Instead, Sergeant O'Dell was waiting for him, straight-backed but grim-faced. "Something wrong, man?" he asked the noncom.

"It's your son, sir. He's not in camp. Neither is Standing Antelope's daughter. They got mounts from the remuda by feeding the guard some bullshit."

The captain's face took on a purple cast. The veins throbbed in his temples, and his fists clenched. "Fred gone? Impossible, man! Impossible!"

"He left this." The noncom handed him a folded sheet of foolscap. The note was folded in thirds, then folded another time.

"Did you read it?"

"No, sir. *Your* name is on it. See?"

"And it was pinned to the lieutenant's tent?"

"No, sir. Pinned to *your* tent. I found it there just a minute ago."

By now the captain had unfolded the paper, and was reading the message. His hands were shaking. O'Dell wondered if he was about to have a seizure.

"Christ!" Leland muttered.

"Sir?"

"I don't want to believe this. But I suppose I'll have to." Then to the sergeant, "Pass the order to the men, we won't be breaking camp. I suppose Melchior Dix's people should be informed too. Fred's gone, all right, and the note explains the reason. Sergeant, go find the scout Ballou and tell him to report, immediately."

"That pair, they've got 'em a long head start, captain. And the weather's looking more and more like rain. Thunderheads on the western peaks. That'll play havoc with tracking. You gonna want to stage a pursuit?"

"That's for me to decide, and I haven't yet weighed all alternatives. I'll let you know. For now, sergeant, you have your orders."

As O'Dell turned and hurried off, Captain Leland fought a sense of confusion at odds with his usual confidence. Fred? His own son do this? With that Indian wench—a red nigger?

Anger seethed in the captain's mind. Anger that threatening to boil over, make him do something rash.

He strode into his tent, kicked over his folding table, dropped into his folding chair.

"Goddamnit," Maynard Leland croaked. His eyes, he found, were leaking tears of frustration.

"Goddamnit to hell!"

Chapter 14

Pike's and McConnell's main wish was to get out of Blackfeet country. Over Starved Man's Pass was the shortest way, but the route was extremely rugged. The mountain men pushed their horses through the long day, getting over their injuries as they put distance between themselves and the braves they'd killed. By the end of the first day, Pike had lost his headache. Skins again had fairly good use of his arm, although some numbness continued to pester him.

By the middle of the second day they were through the pass. But they were still high in the mountains, where the air was chilly and the remains of winter snow blew down from the peaks in white horses' tails. Virgin stands of timber carpeted the slopes. Beyond the close peaks were pockets of mist, concealing distance.

The mountain men guided the bays over spans of rubble and shale, on a trail they'd never traveled before. Escarpments shadowed the ledge, and the way grew narrow, so narrow that the men's legs brushed the rising cliff face. On their right plunged a deep chasm showing the effects of ancient landslides that had dumped whole pine forests.

By late afternoon, iron-gray clouds began to roll in. The comrades were reminded of other mountain storms they'd endured. When lightning started to fork from mountain to mountain, it could be a prelude to tremendous rains. Flash floods could strike without warning. Trails could wash away, trees and boulders could be undercut and start to slide.

Now the thunder rolled like a titanic cannon battery. For the next few minutes the rain held off, but then the downpour began sweeping along the slopes in veils. Pike pulled his collar up and his hat down, hunched his shoulders against the storm and rode on.

McConnell did likewise.

They needed a place to camp, and needed it badly.

The rain was so heavy it obscured the pack horses at the ends of their lead ropes. The mountain men's buckskins were quickly soaked. Temperatures dropped, and Pike and Skins began to shiver.

"Hey, Jack!"

"Yeah?"

"First spot you see that'd offer shelter from this, turn off at it."

"Think I haven't got brains enough? Think you need to tell me that?"

"Jack, we gotta team up on these decisions."

"Like we teamed up when going sheep-hunting? Leaving our Kentucky pistols on the horses' saddles?"

"Aw, Jack. I don't need to hear 'I told you so.' We came out the scrape alive, didn't we?"

"Hope we come through this scrape without catching our death."

It wasn't long after that when Pike noticed a rock jumble just off the trail. Dusk settling in had about made traveling impossible, so the big man turned his horse's nose. There was a hollow in a cliff face, and a substantial rock overhang. Under the overhang and out of the worst of the wind, the mountain man stripped the saddles from the riding horses, the supply bundles from the pack animals. Then he picketed all the horses so they could crop grass.

As the rain continued to pound the Rocky Mountain landscape, Pike and McConnell looked around their campsite for possible rattlesnakes. When the spot got a clean bill of health, Skins said, "There's blown-down tree branches scattered around, some of 'em fairly dry. I'll build us a fire."

"While you're at it, unpack bacon and cornmeal, Skins. I feel like a hot meal. We'll cook up some bannock."

"We?"

"All right, I'll rustle up the bannock myself. But then, I'd also be obliged to eat it myself."

"Swap you the chore of corn-bread frying for the coffee-making."

"You got you a deal."

"Borrow your flint and steel, Jack?"

"Sure. Here."

Fifteen minutes later, the food was cooking over a blaze and the coffee boiling. The mountain men's clothes were hung out to dry on improvised stick frames. Pike and McConnell both sat in front of the flames, shrouded in a wolf skin from the saddle packs, and nothing else. "Warming up, Jack?" Skins asked.

"Doing quite nicely, thanks."

"Any ideas on how to kill the rest of the evening?"

"Now that we're done eating?"

"From now till we get sleepy, yeah."

"Guess I'll leave that up to you," Pike said.

Skins tugged the warm fur hide around him more snugly. "How 'bout spinning a tall tale or two? There's the one about me taking on five Absaroka maidens whose pa, the chief, claimed they hadn't been getting enough. Or better still, why not sing campfire songs? I'll lead off with 'Drink to Me Only With Rum Punch.' "

Pike shifted restlessly inside his wolf skin. "Wait, Skins. I've got another idea. Look."

"What am I s'posed to see?"

"Why, these three walnut shells I'm holding up. Melody Hooper made me a present of 'em."

McConnell's eyes lit up. "The shell game?"

"We can play for a spell right here, on this flat rock."

"What'll we bet?"

"How about our first week's trapping haul, come winter?"

"Best three guesses outa five? All right, Jack, throw down the pea and move the shells around."

Pike won the first play, and followed by winning the next four.

"Damn," McConnell swore. "I been skunked!"

"Skins, let me show you something."

"Is it interesting?"

"For a fella whose got him the gambling habit, it's a vital lesson. I'm going to show exactly how I cheated. Watch now." The big man moved the shells around with blinding speed. Then he turned over the first shell, then the second and the third in turn.

"Jesus," Skins fumed. "No pea under any of 'em."

"Here's the pea," Pike grinned. He held up his hand, to show the pea pressed between his two middle fingers.

"That's how a crooked fella cheats?"

"Well-l-l, a crooked *woman* could do it just about as easy."

"By hiding the pea between the fingers thataway. Damn!"

"You know the old saying, Skins?"

"What's that?"

"The hand, it's quicker than the eye."

Chapter 15

Three days later Pike and McConnell came within sight of the army party's bivouac, set in a disadvantageous undrained swale below a rock face from which run-off from the recent rains had flowed. From fifty yards out, where they'd reined up, not only did the camp appear to be a soggy bog, but the men looked downcast and sullen.

As was customary, the mountain men gave a hail, "Hello, the encampment. Mind if we ride in? It's McConnell and Pike."

Sergeant Patrick O'Dell stood with Melchior Dix beside a clutch of stacked muskets. The noncom and the man of science were deep in conversation. At the sound of the hail, the men turned and waved. "Sure, come on in! First white men not of our bunch we've seen since we left Fort Laramie."

When the mountain men had dismounted the noncom said, "The captain'll likely want to talk, when he gets back."

"He's not in camp? Has he gone out on some chore having to do with making maps?"

"You men don't unnerstand der process," huffed Dix. "On an hex-pedition like this we take sightings, make sketches, record vatt we learn. Back in Washington iss where the maps will actually be drawn. They'll eventually be run off on big printing presses . . ."

O'Dell cut him off. "Since you ask, Pike, you may as well know the truth. Captain Leland's gone off, not for mapmaking, but on a pursuit. A pursuit, as it happens, that matters a great deal to him. He took Muley Ballou and a half-dozen troopers. Been gone three-and-a-half days."

"Pursuit?" Pike said. "You mean like a chase?"

Skins stepped forward, rubbing his numbish arm. "You mean, like in a 'wild-goose chase'?"

O'Dell's smile showed not an ounce of humor. "It appears you've got the captain sized up, right enough. As a matter of fact, our official mission has been getting short shrift lately, ever since the lieutenant left us."

"Which lieutenant?" By now Pike's curiosity was aroused.

But O'Dell wasn't given a chance to answer. "Sergeant!" bellowed a stentorian voice from the other side of the camp. "Over here to me, mister. Now!" Looking around for the one who'd hollered, Pike spotted Lieutenant Meester. The officer's jacket was unbuttoned as sloppily as usual, and the crossed-sabers insignia were askew on his campaign hat.

"Not *that* lieutenant. He remains in charge. Excuse me, gentlemen. I'm being summoned."

Melchior Dix, in his thick European accent, undertook to explain. "It's the *young* Lieutenant Leland who's gone off, ghentlemen, with the Indian woman known as Bright Cloud. She's a pretty maiden, it iss true, and one can see why Fred might haff fallen in love with her. And there does appear to be a real fondness between the pair. I saw the note he pinned to his father's tent when he made up his mind to leave. Do you know, he actually plans to marry the girl!"

Pike glanced at McConnell.

McConnell returned the glance.

"Marry her? Where, in one of the white folks' settlements?"

The scientist shook his white-haired head. "That iss the amazingk part, ghentlemen. The young couple wish to take part in an authentic tribal ceremony of the Shoshone people, in a Shoshone village. That's where they've headed."

"Whew," McConnell grunted. "Ain't that something?"

"Jesus," Pike said. "The Shoshone lands are off to the southwest. Young Leland and Bright Cloud, they'll need to pass right through dangerous Blackfeet country!"

"I suppose you'll want to camp with us tonight?"

The officer talking to the mountain men was pompous, arrogant, almost hostile. Gower Meester's fiery, sunburned face was slack as putty and he tended to look past Pike and McConnell as he rapped out his words.

100

"Oh, not really," Pike said. "We just happened to see your camp, and dropped in to say hello. Reckon we'll bed down for the night on yonder hillside. In the morning we'll be on our way."

"Acceptable." The lieutenant, his greeting of the arrivals considered finished, stalked off to his tent.

Sergeant O'Dell shrugged. "I won't apologize for my superior officer. I think you gents know where I really stand. Were it me, I'd act more inviting to civilian travelers."

"Officers will be officers," the mountain man said. "I learned that long ago, which is why I try not to have truck with 'em. Well, we'll be going now, having stock to water. After that, we'll be spreading our bedrolls." But as he turned to the horses he glimpsed a man sitting on the ground, his wrists secured in heavy manacles. "By the way, O'Dell, isn't that fella the same one as took that flogging back at Laramie?"

"That's him."

"Got himself in more trouble?"

"Hell, Pike, maybe it's best to tell you the whole story. Sure, part of it's the love affair between the captain's son and Standing Antelope's daughter. But there's more. Seems Lieutenant Fred and Bright Cloud were seen 'doing it' by Brubaker. Blackmail came naturally to his criminal mind."

"Blackmail?"

"Blackmail. Brubaker knew—as everyone on this expedition knows—the contempt Fred's father holds for all Indians. So Brubaker went to Fred, told him money would buy his silence. But young Leland, rather than pay, simply ran off with Bright Cloud. The thing came to light with Fred's farewell note to his father. The captain lost no time in clamping the private in irons. His idea is to have Brubaker court-martialed when we get back to a real army station.''

Brubaker, Pike saw, was more than merely morose as he sat there in chains. His confined hands shook with suppressed fury, and his unshaven face was beset by nervous tics.

''Blackmail's a more serious offense than gun-stealing?''

O'Dell shrugged. ''Well, it certainly had more effect on the captain, from a personal point of view. And there's a compounding of the racial angle—you can see from the private's complexion that he's part Indian. I think Captain Leland plans to make a case for incorrigibility.''

''Incor—?'' McConnell started to ask.

''He means,'' Pike explained, ''that this Brubaker can't learn to keep his hands clean. C'mon, Skins, it's not our concern, the running off of an army shavetail. Let's get the horses to grass and rustle us up a bite of supper.''

A few minutes later they rode out of the encampment. A few troopers in blue took notice, but most didn't.

Brubaker merely sat on the ground, scowling. Now, who're them two mountain men? he wondered. What d'they want here? Damn 'em, they're free as birds, whilst I sit here in chains.

I'm gonna be free too! So maybe I won't be able to find ol' Milt and team up to make money. Instead, I can go look up my kin among the Blackfeet. Shit, I ain't one t'be took back east for trial. Yeah, my Blackfeet kin, Angry Bear's band! It had been quite a while since he'd sentimentalized about the notorious war leader. But just now, since they were expert in killing Long Knives, he and his warriors became first in the heart of Orlo.

Hell, I oughtta be a killer of Long Knives too! The Lelands, and the rest. Yeah, kill, kill, KILL! The confined trooper, with thin lips writhing, kept on mouthing the word, "Kill." And when the night fell, he was still mumbling it.

"Kill! Kill all Long Knife sons of bitches! Kill 'em!"

Night came, and Pike and McConnell rolled up their soogans, falling asleep quickly after the long day in the saddle. The campfire coals cooled to a cherry glow, the riding mounts and pack horses went right on cropping grama. Midnight came and went, the loudest sounds in the campsite the rustling of field mice and the snores of the two mountain men. Then suddenly, the silence was broken by a shout of alarm from the direction of the army encampment.

"Hey!"

"Goddamn son of a bitch!"

"The prisoner, men. He's out of his chains and missing. Turn out of your bedrolls, grab your muskets and find the no-account bastard."

Pike and McConnell leaped to their feet, just in time to see a huge, dark shape hurtling toward them out of the night. Pike's first move had been to snatch up his Hawken, and now he threw it to his shoulder, tracking the hurtling shape of the horseman. Approaching hoofbeats drummed the turf. But before tearing into Pike's and Skins's camp the horse swerved, and then a second horse—running on a lead rope—also swerved.

"You gonna shoot, Jack, or get off the pot?"

"Can't risk it, Skins. Don't know who the rider might be. This night's a damned dark one!"

Then the rider was gone, the dust settling. McConnell held a dry branch to the coals of the fire, igniting a crude torch. Then, walking over to look at the rider's trail, he called out, "Hey, Jack . . . This you got to see!"

Pike walked over and joined him. "So, what did you find?"

"Couple of interesting things. This kepi cap, like soldiers wear. And this."

"Oh-oh," said Pike. What Skins was holding up in his good left hand was a musket, standard army issue. "Looks like Private Brubaker's up to his old tricks again. Stealing guns. Just hope the ones he got this time don't get into the wrong hands."

"Like?"

"The Blackfeet are always dangerous. But with even a few 'thunder sticks'—which most of 'em still believe are magic—well, these mountains could turn into hell for white folks!"

Chapter 16

"Brubaker *what?* Got out of his chains how?"

Skins McConnell looked dumbfounded because he *was* dumbfounded.

O'Dell held his palms up to McConnell and Pike and shrugged. "You spend your years in this man's army, you see it happening too often. Combine a wily rascal and a careless guard and . . . But do I really need to tell it again, McConnell?"

They were standing in the firelit troopers' encampment. "Let *me* try, sergeant," Pike said. "I know it's hard to believe, Skins, but you met some of the outfit's recruits. They're green! Greener'n Lemhi Valley in springtime. What O'Dell said, Skins, was that Brubaker sold the night sentry on a lie. Claimed he had the chills and shits, and when the man came close, Orlo coldcocked him and got the key to the manacles."

"That I understand," Skins said. "But Jack, the sarge said Orlo got rifles and a horse. Well, sure, there's the remuda, and it was nighttime and all, but guns?"

"This is a typical bivouac, and soldiers aren't mountain men. When in camp, they don't keep their guns close by 'em. You saw this afternoon, Skins, the muskets were stacked in the center of the ring of tents. With everybody asleep, Brubaker snuck off with all he could tote, loaded him up a pack horse. The alarm wasn't given till he rode out."

"Yeah, I see it now. Too bad the Shoshones were made to camp so far from the main bivouac."

"Captain Leland's policy," O'Dell explained.

"I figured as much."

Pike, listening, put his ear to a tall alder's trunk. "Aha! The troopers and Standing Antelope's braves, the ones who gave chase. They're riding back, I hear their horses coming. And here's Lieutenant Meester, riding in the lead."

Meester stepped from leather and glared about. "Well, the half-breed's vanished. Rode into a stream bed, couldn't be tracked."

"The chief of Long Knives speaks true," confirmed Standing Antelope. "This Brubaker knows how to cover his trail."

"He's gone then," Pike asked.

The Indian thumped his chest. "Much gone. It is said that he is half-Blackfoot. This I believe."

Meester tugged off gauntlets, slapped them against his thigh. "No further orders, Sergeant O'Dell. I'll study on matters the rest of the night. Maybe the captain'll be back in the morning."

He went inside his tent, but didn't light his candle lantern.

"Funny, isn't it?" Jack Pike observed. "How an officer and a gentleman can be so damned *un*gentleman-like!''

Orlo Brubaker rode like hell through the night. Whenever the lead horse wanted to balk, the deserter yanked on the line roughly and the ridden chestnut and pack animal just kept galloping hard along the mountain trails. Since splashing into that first stream to foil pursuit, Orlo had worked hard at concealing his tracks. He'd chosen the rockiest terrain, and when forced to cross soft ground he'd stop and dismount, then go back and brush out hoof prints with tree branches.

He was feeling good about his escape from the army encampment. Captain Leland had given him a rough time, because the blackmail try on his son had driven Fred off. But that was all behind Orlo now, had been since he'd clubbed Private Hans Bischoff with his manacles.

To keep himself fired up, Brubaker kept cursing Captain Leland as he rode—Lieutenant Leland, and every army officer he'd ever come in contact with.

He was glad to be a deserter, glad to have made off with a dozen or so soldiers' muskets.

''Hot damn! Now this coon's free as a mountain man!''

When the sun came up, he planned to cut north-west over Big Badger Pass, and once into the rugged mountains beyond he could expect to start encountering Blackfeet bands. Before then, of course, he'd have shucked the rest of his uniform. He'd already flung away the detested cap.

The safest way was entering Blackfeet territory naked as a jay, clean of any and all White Eyes paraphernalia.

"And, old hoss," he shouted gleefully to the roan he straddled, "come daylight, whilst you're drinkin' at a stream we come to, I'll be puttin' the bank mud, fire ashes, and wildberry juice to use! The best use. Smearin' myself with stripes and patterns. For to paint me in war paint, Blackfeet-style!"

The talking to himself went on as he rode. "I figure ol' Angry Bear, he'll be glad to see me again. The fella as left the tribe years back as a younker, but now's seen his mistake. That's what I think, hoss. I'm bringin' news to the chief 'bout the Long Knives on Fly Creek. Their outfit's short on guns, long on weakstick civilians and hired Shoshone help!

"When Angry Bear hears, he'll go kill-crazy. And won't Orlo Brubaker be pleased as punch to join the war party sent out.

"Hell, and I won't call m'self Brubaker no more, neither. My new name'll be my old Blackfoot one—Poison Snake!"

Chapter 17

Fred Leland and Bright Cloud rode the mountain maze, aboard sure-footed, mountain-bred ponies. The mounts that they'd "borrowed" from Standing Antelope without his permission. Now the couple followed age-old game trails, always southwesterly toward the safe Shoshone range.

Yesterday Bright Cloud had told Fred their destination, the village of Chief Buffalo Tail. It would make her happy, she said, to be married there. Old friends she'd grown up with would turn out to wish her well, and help set up and furnish hers and her husband's lodge with cooking kettles, furs for beds and other necessities.

Since the couple had left the expedition's camp, four days had elapsed. The country they passed through grew ever more magnificent, more awe-inspiring. But the mountain terrain was also rugged, and the trails were curving, precipitous, risky.

It was the afternoon of another cloudless day, and the trail they rode wound in the shadows of imposing massifs, zigged and zagged along perpendicular canyon walls. Now Bright Cloud, in the lead, turned on her saddle pad to signal Fred, pointing.

Fred called, "What is it, Bright Cloud? What do you see?"

"Down there. A valley we must cross."

And indeed, they soon rode a descending slope. To the west lay a high, knob-like rock dome, and in the valley's depths wound the silver thread of a stream.

To reach the water the man and woman would need to pick their way. And Fred Leland was thirsty.

Damned thirsty.

And yet, when he spotted an unusual kind of bush, he reined in. "Hold on, Bright Cloud. A new specimen—a real find!" From under his blue officer's blouse he whipped a notebook, and on a blank page he began to sketch. The lines he drew showed the twining trunk, the shapes of leaves. Finally, he noted the location with regard to nearby peaks. "Damn!" the officer blurted. "I'll have to guess at the altitude. Had to leave the barometer behind, too bulky to transport, plus I couldn't bring myself to steal government property."

Bright Cloud smiled, indulging her man.

Fred was ready to move on, and now the couple rode closer together. The way down into the valley was steep, and the trail was broken with frequent switchbacks. First the horses smelled the water, then Leland caught sight of it, a sparkling band of blue.

"I think I need a rest stop."

The young Shoshone beauty agreed. "Yes, the horses need rest, too. And a drink."

"Bright Cloud, I love you."

She had only a vague notion of what a white man meant by love. Still, she answered, "Fred, I love you too."

When the ponies were picketed and grazing, the couple flopped on the stream bank. Lying flat, Fred drank deeply of the sweet water. Then, "Come, Bright Cloud. Sit beside me."

She came, sat, and nestled against him. He looked down, admiring his future bride. He saw in her high spirits, the black eyes aglow with the pure joy of being alive. In her hand-worked garments, colorful with trader's beads, she looked clean-limbed, healthy, lovely.

He took her small, strong hand. "Maybe we'll camp here for a few days, wife-to-be. It's a nice spot, isn't it, wife-to-be? I've noticed more than a few unusual plant species I should make notes on. You understand why I go on making notes on flora and fauna, don't you? It's the scientific bent in me that I can't shake, that just seems to be part of me."

"I think I understand," she said. She really didn't, though. Fred had shown her several of the strange objects that the White Eyes called books. Some contained pictures such as he, himself, was always drawing, pictures of large trees and tiny plants, and all the leaf types meticulously shown. One book contained pictures of animals. But the more Bright Cloud thought about it, the more it seemed the plants and animals would always be found in the same old places. Anyone who wanted to could look at the real thing. So why make books?

Now Fred was telling her, "I think we should stay here for a few days. It could prove most profitable."

At that her pretty face grew serious. "This is Blackfeet country, Fred. Blackfeet are fierce warriors, and they hate all White Eyes. And my people, the Shoshones, are their enemies from the grandfather times. If the Blackfeet come upon us here, they'll kill us."

Fred's lips brushed her copper cheek. "Aw, hostile redskins won't find us. I possess the Leland luck!"

"Luck?"

"Er, what Indians call power. Medicine."

"Medicine?"

"We're protected from harm, you and me, Bright Cloud. Plus I've got several firearms with me, something the Blackfeet don't have. I'm an expert with my Kentucky pistol, you know. Look, I'll show you. Watch! Time for target practice."

He drew his pistol from his belt, and pulled back the hammer. He squinted, sighting at a pine cone on a tree.

The woman, ashy-faced, begged him, "Don't shoot! The thunder stick's bark, it could bring enemies here. Many enemies."

He lowered the gun. "Bright Cloud, you worry too much. When we get among your own people, will you stop fretting?"

She looked up at him, dark eyes aglow. "I'll stop as soon as we're safe, Fred. I promise."

"Meanwhile, I've got a way to take your mind off things."

She glanced around. She knew he wanted her body,

as much as she wanted his. But she was more than a little edgy about the Blackfeet.

Bright Cloud spoke. "You want to make the dark pleasure with me? Now? Out in the open? In daylight?"

"All those things. Here goes, Bright Cloud. Hang on and follow Fred, the lover boy!"

Leland enfolded the woman in his arms, pressed his lips to hers. They kissed with ardor. Bright Cloud sighed when he palmed her small, firm breast. Leland's member, swollen, strained for its freedom. Unbidden, the woman's fingers roamed, found the bulge that strained his pants fly.

"Oh, Fred!" Her sweet voice cracked. Leland dipped a hand down inside her neckline, caressed one hemisphere, which made Bright Cloud gasp. "But, the Blackfeet . . ."

"Screw the Blackfeet! Or better, why don't I just screw you!" He stretched the woman on the grass, leaned over her. "My pants buttons. My belt. Undo 'em? Take off my trousers?"

Soon all the garments were off his pale-skinned frame. As she'd worked at his clothes, he'd worked at hers. She was naked now, a strong bronze goddess.

He lowered himself against the woman, a heady aroma arising to tease his nostrils. He felt below, and stroked her soft, furred bush, then proceeded to her cleft. He found it a drooling pot of warm, slick honey. With finger and thumb he parted soft folds, found her ready for his gift.

His engorged manhood plowed her belly, and she loved it. He moved his club-haft between her thighs, as her steaming cave yawned to accept him. She could feel the soft grass against her buttocks and shoulder blades, and then she felt the man, and shivered with first contact.

Fred slid into Bright Cloud's passage, every nuance of sensation honed. The man trembled and quaked, as did she as she accepted his long cock. The raging sounds of their enjoyment melded with the splashing and bubbling of the playful stream. She started to whimper as her cavern pulsed. Tremor after tremor flowed between the lovers as they rose to heights of erotic bliss.

Their act went on for a long, long time. Finally Fred Leland gasped audibly, starting the long coast to completion. With grunts and cries they thrashed and crushed the grass.

Bright Cloud and her man came together, a shattering occasion. She was gored asunder with delight.

As the shudders of enjoyment abated and the joyous couple's heartbeats slowed, they stretched out on the bank of the stream. Fred lay back, looking up at the tree canopy. A contented smile fixed his chiseled lips. How this unschooled Indian girl sensed his needs! How she applied herself! He felt grateful, blessed.

She lay at his side, her pert breasts pressed to him. She too was satisfied.

"We should be going soon," she said.

"A bit more rest?"

"Well-l-l, a little bit, maybe."

The horses' *chomp-chomping* was a relaxing sound.

Fred couldn't decide whether to sleep, or couple again with the willing woman.

He pondered how content he was with his mate. And how, for the two of them, things would always stay this way.

He felt he was the luckiest of the lucky Lelands.

Why shouldn't his good fortune—and Bright Cloud's—go right on holding?

Chapter 18

Pike was rubbing down his rangy bay with grass, and the mount appreciated it. "Like my pappy told me when I was a pup," he muttered, "take care of your horse and your horse'll take care of you."

It was a motto that had served him in good stead since the big man had drifted west to become a trapper in the Rockies.

The country out here was beautiful, but it could be dangerous country—a true killer land for those who weren't strong and didn't know its ways.

Jack Pike was strong, all right—one of the biggest, whang-leather-tough men who'd ever trod the mountain trails, ever stood atop a wind-swept rimrock looking down on golden eagles that soared there with wings outstretched. And Pike knew the mountains' ways, too, as well any white man could or would. That was the reason he took good care of his horse.

Of his guns.

Of his saddle and all his other equipment.

A fella was a damned fool to count on luck alone

for survival in this vast wilderness that was the Rocky Mountain Range. Pike had seen plenty of those who'd done so wind up dead—or a lot worse than dead!

Assuredly, Pike knew, there were worse things than death. Seeing loved ones killed was one. Another was finding oneself being put to long, drawn-out torture by the most vicious experts at it there were.

The bloody-handed Blackfeet were expert at dishing out death, both instant death and slow death filled to the brim with horrible agonies. This had been so for as long as anyone could remember.

And now there was a new element in the game. Orlo Brubaker. Obviously the guns the half-breed had stolen when deserting weren't all for his own use. The use of his Blackfeet "brothers," then? Pike's hunch was that Orlo would try to get even with the army that he hated so much.

Skins McConnell called out, "Hey Jack, you reckon it's true? What Hans said, Hans the sentry? That Brubaker bragged about the Blackfoot blood in his veins? That he made a vow what he'd do when he got out in the mountains? That he'd be stirring up the tribe against the Long Knives?"

Pike finished up with his horse, patted its rump and let it return to grazing. "I believe the story, Skins, because it sounds plumb true. Private Bischoff may have gotten fooled because he was green, but he heard what he heard. And from what I've seen of Orlo, the man is meaner than a sidewinder and twice as dangerous. Why, with the ax he's got to grind against the army . . ."

"A hard time's on its way to these mountains?"

"C'rect!"

"Oh, shit," McConnell said. "Here comes the ossifer, tramping this way!"

For some reason unfathomable to Pike, his friend had taken to calling Maynard Leland "the ossifer." The captain and his search party had returned less then an hour ago, and already the straight, stiff-backed captain was crossing the distance between his tent and the camp of the mountain men.

Captain Leland had sent a messenger over to Pike earlier, requesting Pike's presence at his tent. Pike had ignored the summons. Was the officer's visit now prompted by that?

"Christ, Jack," McConnell was saying. "Just look at that blond mustache bristle. The ossifer, he seems madder'n a starved hog on election day!"

"I'm not in the army," Pike reminded his friend. "When a command's given, it ain't my habit to jump to it."

No sooner than Pike said this, the captain came up to stand before him. Leland was as neat as ever, with his uniform freshly sponged of dust, his campaign hat set dead-level. His voice carried its usual haughty ring, "Pike, when I rode in, Lieutenant Meester informed me of your presence. I sent for you, but you chose to ignore it."

"Now, why would you be wanting me, captain? You've got Muley Ballou."

"Whom I hired, I remind you, to be my guide after *you,* Pike, turned the job down."

The big mountain man snorted. "Muley's the wet-

118

test drunk between here and the Missouri bottoms. You could've done a heap better.''

"I hired the best white man available at the time!"

"I was going to say, you could've done better by using Standing Antelope as your head scout and guide."

A soaring cinder speck rode the high sky. A buzzard, Pike knew. Was its appearance at this particular time an omen?

Captain Leland's face had grown a shade redder. His lips trembled with the outrage he seemed to feel. "Put that much trust in a miserable red heathen? I could never do it!"

"Couldn't . . . or *wouldn't?"*

"Tell 'im, Jack," Skins mouthed. "Attaway!"

Leland said, "I'd like to come to my point, mister." The topographer was working to control himself.

"Well, since you hiked all the way over here, you may as well go on ahead."

"You'll listen? Good. If not for me, for the sake of my son. My absent son."

"I recall hearing something about your son's hotfooting it. Your son, weren't you pissed at him?"

"Because his ambition was to become a squaw man? Pike, don't you know about old Eastern families like ours? Families with social status? Fred is my son. Fred is a Leland of the social-register New York Lelands!"

Pike and Skins shook their heads in unison. McConnell decided to butt in, "A question, ossif—er, captain. Let me see if I catch your drift. You want the kid back? Does that mean all's forgiven? And it's fine with you now, having Bright Cloud for a daughter-in-law?''

Leland quivered like a clanging hearth poker. ''I'm not saying anything of the kind! But Fred is my son. When he grew to manhood after his mother died, I used influence to get him into West Point. He attended the United States Military Academy, McConnell, and he thrived!''

Pike posed the next question. ''Thrived at swordsmanship, riding into battle, that kind of stuff?''

For the first time, the captain's shoulders went less than square. ''Actually, no,'' Maynard admitted with voice less assured. ''Why I'm telling you this I don't know, desperation, perhaps. What Fred excelled at was academic courses. Book-learning, especially science. Why, the lad's turned into a top-notch cartographer and navigator. Plus, he's a genius at art.''

Skins wondered, ''Cart . . . ? Nav . . . ?''

Pike said, ''So he can make maps, find his way by the stars, draw pictures. But now he's a lieutenant in the army, and obviously a man. He bedded a hot-blooded woman—Indian women *are* that way, y'know—and made her like it. Then he ran off with her to join her people. Followed in the footsteps of the white men who've done it before, a tough, feisty sort. I'd say Fred Leland has real gumption.''

''I want him back,'' Leland barked, again in a parade-ground voice.

Pike shook his head. ''Don't know as you can have him back, Captain. Fred's a grown-up man now. He's taken him a woman. He won't kowtow to his pa any more! *And* he's a deserter from the United States Army."

"Don't go on! For God's sake, don't go on!" The Captain looked devastated, which surprised Pike some. There were age lines at the eye- and mouth-corners. His frame, backdropped by the camp tents, seemed to be slumped.

"Pike," Leland said, "I'm going to sit down. Here on the grass."

"I'd suggest looking out for horse turds, Captain."

Leland smiled ruefully. "Good advice. Thanks."

He pulled out a pipe—a short-stemmed corncob—and after a few minutes had it stoked and was puffing energetically. With his smoke drifting off downwind, he spoke. "Look at it this way, Pike. Take my offer and *I'll* personally foot the bill, not the army. Without the government being involved, you'll have free rein. Free rein to find my son. So he's traveling with a Shoshone girl? I admit, she likely knows Indian survival skills. But Fred is still a child in many ways, a babe in the woods."

"Hmm," Pike said. "A babe in the woods. Woods hereabouts are full of prowling Blackfeet."

"Look," Leland said. "I just returned from leading a search party after Fred and Bright Cloud. Ballou was our scout. We not only lost the trail, we *got* lost! Ballou's only half-competent, at best." Leland puffed his pipe some more. "Going on that patrol taught me something. Finding Fred isn't something the army can do. That's why I've come to you, Pike. Fred mustn't die! Not because of a stupid misunderstanding. So, Pike and McConnell, take my money for finding Fred and the girl. Bring 'em both to me, wherever the expedition is by then.'' He laughed. ''You'll have little trouble finding us, I'll bet.''

Now Leland's voice rose again. ''Here's my promise, Pike. Bring my son to me and I'll sit down with him, talk over reasonably the genteel life he's forfeiting. Appeal to him. After that, if still he wants the girl, he can go and live out his life with her tribe.''

''It hurts you, Fred's marrying red?''

A nod. ''It hurts.''

''He's right, Jack,'' Skins offered. ''The shavetail *is* a babe in the woods. Like in the fairy tale.''

Pike looked down at Maynard Leland sternly. ''I see something clearer than I did, captain. It's sound what you say. I'm thinking.

Sure, the expedition can go on with its work—you've close to thirty men, not counting Shoshones. That's enough to fight off all but the biggest war parties. Tell you what! I'll take the job. And Skins will come along to back me. Right, Skins?''

''Right.''

Pike went on. ''The deal will be as you outlined, Captain. We'll get Fred out of trouble and keep him out. The same goes for Bright Cloud. And when we bring in the couple, there'll be no forcing 'em. You won't threaten Fred with disinheriting him, or arrest him on the desertion charge.''

Leland stood up, weary but relieved. ''Never fear, gentlemen. My son will be free. Free as Orlo Brubaker is now.''

Pike smiled. ''I like your example.''

Leland smiled back. ''I thought you might.''

Maynard Leland began walking off, and already McConnell was muttering. "Never figured to go to work for the ossifer. Jack, you reckon the ossifer, he'll keep his word?"

Pike shrugged. "I doubt the Captain will send his kid to an army brig. But so what if it happens? You and me, we'd just help Fred to pull an Orlo Brubaker!"

Chapter 19

The next morning Pike and McConnell rolled out of their soogans, relieved their bowels and bladders, and had breakfast coffee at the boil, all before the brightening of the brief false dawn. Pike aimed to get an early start after the missing Fred Leland and Bright Cloud, but it appeared as if the weather wouldn't be cooperating. Dark clouds hung over the western peaks, and the lightning behind them forked and flickered ominously.

Pike performed his routine morning check of weapons, polishing any rust from the Green River knife and tomahawk, applying bear grease to the gun-locks of the Hawken rifle and the Kentucky pistol. As he picked up his powder horn to fresh-prime the long gun, he asked "What do you think, Skins? Will the rain hold off?"

McConnell studied the mist-shrouded mountain's flanks. "Till around midday, maybe. What's your own guess, Jack?"

"We'll be lucky if we ride dry even that long."

"Thought you didn't take account of luck."

"I don't," Pike affirmed. "But I know you do."

"You still joshing me about all my gambling losses?"

"Well, you thought shell games had to be honest."

"See! You're joshing! Damn you, Jack!"

"And you don't think it's fair, if I want to josh?"

"No, Jack. I don't."

"Then I'll quit. How's that for true friendship?"

Finished with the Hawken, Pike took up the pistol. He tipped fine priming powder from his horn to the pan. "By the way, Skins, before we pull stakes this forenoon, I want another talk with Standing Antelope."

"Again?"

"Again. He may have a notion about where his daughter might be headed with our shavetail-turned-white-Indian, Fred. A notion the chief didn't let on to the captain."

"Or Muley Ballou?"

Pike spat on the ground between his oversized moccasins. "Who would tell Ballou anything? He's not only an asshole, as a guide up here he's a damned fraud."

"Well, I wouldn't tell him anything," Skins said. "And not you, either."

"Nor would Standing Antelope, who's one right smart Indian."

Ten minutes later, Pike was standing with the chief in his tepee. The Shoshone wore a solemn, even gloomy, face. The mountain man spoke in a voice that was low, yet urgent. "So, Standing Antelope, here's how it stands. Your daughter has gone off with a White Eyes, a man new to these mountains, a greenhorn. A man like that could slow an Indian woman down plenty. Why, the couple might even end up in trouble.''

Standing Antelope nodded. ''That is so. I did not know they were going until they were gone, He-Whose-Head-Touches-the-Sky. Huh! Bright Cloud with Le-land, young subchief of the Long Knives! Well, the pair are young and have hot blood, which will help them to make strong sons some day.'' He was quiet for a moment, and then went on. ''Bright Cloud and Le-land, they go now to a village of Sho-shone people.''

''Chief, that's what I got to find out. Where, exactly? Any idea *which* village?''

''There are many villages. Bright Cloud will pick one.''

''The Shoshone lands, they're a long way from here. It's wild country up that way, full of bears, wolves and other mean critters. Also full of Black-feet.''

The man with bronze skin nodded, and the feather in his hair bobbed. ''The Blackfeet and the Shoshone, they're enemies. For just two people, a man and a woman, to ride through their lands, the risk is great. I could have sent warriors along to protect Bright Cloud. But her heart was given to old Le-land's son.''

''I understand, chief. Bright Cloud couldn't tell you her plans, because if you'd known, Captain Leland would've fired you from your job.''

"Fired, He-Whose-Head-Touches-the-Sky? What does my brother mean by 'fired'?"

"It's a white man's term. Means 'send you away.' "

The chief looked up at Pike, the taller man. "Here's the way it is, Bright Cloud has chosen the man that she wants. She will be safe with him—I can only hope."

"And you've no idea which Shoshone headman's village she'll pick to be married in?"

Standing Antelope thought a bit. His brow furrowed and his hawk nose twitched. Finally: "She has kin in all the villages. But she's always liked the head of one clan most, old Chief Buffalo Tail. Does He-Whose-Head-Touches-the-Sky know Buffalo Tail?"

A nod.

"Buffalo Tail's third wife, she is sister to Standing Antelope's second wife. And now that he thinks on it, Standing Antelope is sure! Yes, I think Bright Cloud will go to Buffalo Tail! In the valley under Big Tree Mountain, He-Whose-Head-Touches-the-Sky!" Then the chief turned his head, glanced at Pike sidelong. "Of course, Standing Antelope's medicine might be weak, his guess wrong about this."

"Don't worry, my brother," Pike reassured the Indian. "I and my friend, we'll ask in every Shoshone village till we find the pair."

"That is good, He-Whose-Head-Touches-the-Sky."

"It is good, Standing Antelope." Then Pike turned to go. "And thanks chief. You've been a help. A big help!"

On his way back through the bivouac, Pike met Muley Ballou. The buckskins of the so-called scout

127

stank, so did the man. And so did his breath, when he started talking. "So, mountain man, you're goin' hunting? For the shavetail and the squaw? Well, I wish you no success! I failed, and you're no better'n me."

Pike started to push past him. "I've no quarrel with you, Ballou. But I'm in a hurry."

"Cap'n Leland, he told me th' score! You'll be ridin' out today, you and your damned-fool side-kick!"

"Ballou, watch what you call McConnell. He's not a damned fool."

"I was at Laramie last month, same time as you! McConnell almost got hisself cleaned out, dint he? By the late shell-game cheat?"

This remark caught Pike's interest. *'Late* cheat? Handy Hooper's dead, then?"

"Killed by Blackfeet. A turrible way to go. Just found out about it days ago our li'l chase party after Fred. We found the corpse. 'Twas nothin' but an arrow pincushion!" Ballou's grimace showed brown, rotten teeth.

Pike tried to reconstruct what happened. "He must've tried to get through to Fort Bridger. Alone."

Ballou belched, then giggled. "Looks thataway. Things got hot at Laramie, he had to go someplace. Didn't have no ass to peddle, not like his sweet sis did."

Pike's fist slammed hard to Ballou's midsection, doubling the scout. His mangy badger-fur cap flew, as the man went staggering back, gasping. "Melody Hooper, she's, fine woman!" So saying, Pike threw an uppercut, sending Ballou back into a pup tent, collapsing it. A couple of army privates nearby gawked. Muley Ballou lay squirming on the ground, groaning.

Pike turned on his heel and strode up the hill. McConnell had the horses saddled and packed.

The mountains thrust up gray heads under the lowering sky. Pike felt the wind—a chilly, damp wind—slice through his buckskins.

No need for good-byes, not to the elder Leland, nor Sergeant O'Dell or Melchior Dix, the old scientist with the snow-white hair.

Pike knew what his job was, and the danger involved.

It was time to get started.

Chapter 20

Orlo Brubaker—or, as he had taken to calling himself again, Poison Snake—made his way down the steep, treacherous trail from the canyon rimrock, taking handholds on clumpy plant stalks, and footholds where they could be found on loose talus. He managed to move silently, drawing on skills acquired in his Indian boyhood, and although he was edgy at the prospect of rejoining the Blackfeet, he knew that his best chance for revenge on the army lay with his savage "brothers."

The horses he'd brought, one still laden with more than a dozen stolen soldiers' muskets, were picketed to a scrub pinyon up behind him on the rim. Below lay the large village of skin-covered lodges that he'd ridden so hard to get to.

Orlo could see scores of Blackfeet women working and gossiping among the dwellings and in the central ceremonial area, the playing children, the band's many dogs. The half-breed presumed most of the warriors would be off hunting—most, but not all.

He'd already sneaked past several hard-faced look-outs posted on the canyon rim, thanking his luck that *they* hadn't spotted *him*. Orlo's plan was to get into the village proper, talk to the band's leaders and inform them that he, who'd been raised among the Blackfeet, wanted to rejoin the tribe. That made clear, he'd go on to outline how he, due to having lived among the White Eyes for a time, could help the band make successful war on the hated Long Knives.

Of course, he might not be able to get his message across. The tribesmen, always temperamental and unpredictable, could easily kill him before he got the chance.

One minute he was feeling good, the next, not so good. The two squat, powerful warriors came out of a rock jumble behind Orlo, one grabbing him by his greasy hair, the other thrusting a knife point to his throat.

"Who are you? What are you doing here?" one of the braves hissed fiercely. Talking the Blackfeet language sounded like gargling with a mouthful of pebbles.

Brubaker thought he knew why they were holding off killing him. He'd daubed himself generously with the paint he'd contrived, mostly brown creek mud and reddish berry juice. And now, to impress his captors, he managed some words in the old, half-forgotten language of his boyhood. "I came to see Angry Bear," he said slurringly. "Take me to your chief."

The pair got on either side of him, starting him marching. They had their tomahawks out. Orlo had no choice but to act brave.

He didn't want to die.

He put on a good performance.

"Christ, Pike! We're riding in a goddamned downpour!"

"Has the thunder made you deaf?"

"Almost!"

"Has the lightning blown you from the saddle?"

"It will!"

"You ain't cold are you?"

"You're goddamned right I'm cold!"

The cloudburst had swept down out of the peaks with roaring fury, but Pike had elected to push on. He felt a stong sense of urgency about his and Skins's mission, that he'd best find Fred Leland before the shavetail got himself into serious danger.

Lightning was sheeting from horizon to horizon, and thunder cannonaded until the ground shook under the horses' hooves.

"This plan of yours better work out, Jack," Skins called out. "Better help us gain ground on Fred and Bright Cloud."

"Well, if you think about it, Skins, this is a good time to ride this country. In fact, it's a damned good time."

McConnell gritted his teeth, squinted against the hard-blowing, stinging raindrops. "Oh?"

"Won't the Blackfeet be holed up out of the weather, scared shitless of their gods of thunder and lightning? While they're kowtowing to their superstitions, they're not out here fixing to lift our scalps."

McConnell grinned. "Y'know, Jack, sometimes you make a lotta sense."

"I know," Pike said. "I know."

Then the most reverberating thunderclap yet made it seem like the mountains were falling down.

Pike clapped heels to the stolid bay's sides, and led the way into the heart of the tempest's fury. The rain drummed and punished the men, but the sun was shining somewhere.

They only had to find the rainbow and the treasure that lay at its end. Fred Leland and Bright Cloud, the missing ones.

As Orlo Brubaker was ushered into the presence of the Blackfoot chief. He recognized the tough, older warrior as Angry Bear himself. But as he peered into that haughty, hawk-nosed visage, he realized that with one false step his scalp would be dangling from the lodgepole overhead.

The man in the buffalo-horn headdress and bear-claw necklace had glinting eyes of obsidian, and from under beetling brows they glared out at the half-breed. Angry Bear was spoken to by the lookouts who'd caught the intruder, but the broad, brown face showed not a trace of change—until he absorbed the fact that Orlo spoke the language of "The People."

"You speak our tongue?" he rumbled as he scowled.

"Yes, Angry Bear."

"You know how I am called? How comes this?"

"Well, for openers, chief, I was born in this very

canyon, just a short walk from where we're standing. My mother was a woman of your clan, my father a white trader who passed through, swapping beads and blankets for the tribe's furs. Maybe you remember me. I am called Brubaker by the White Eyes I went away to live among, but who I now hate. I sure do hope you remember me, Angry Bear. In my youth I was called Poison Snake.''

"I remember no young man called Poison Snake.'' Turning to the warriors who pinned Orlo's arms, "My brothers, take this one to the ceremonial circle, let him be put to death. Slow death. Let his screams of great pain go on a long, long time!'' The chief snorted with contempt. "Why, how foolish he is! Trying to paint himself like us, but not getting the patterns quite right! Yes, death to this foolish one!''

Orlo's heart pounded against his ribs, and cold sweat sheened his skin. He knew he'd need to talk fast, else he'd be staked out on an anthill or to a butchering stake.

"Wait, Angry Bear!'' he blurted. "I can be useful to your band! I've brung a small bunch of thunder sticks for you and your warriors! Gifts! And can I teach you how to use 'em! Plus I know about some Long Knives that've snuck into your territory. I can help you find 'em, kill 'em, get the rest of their thunder sticks. Then you can raise *real* hell among all the White Eyes startin' to come through these parts!''

The chief now stood impassively, eyes fixed away from the pinioned captive. "Away with him!'' With one hand he pointed toward the center of the village, while with the other he brushed his chest and the ugly

134

scars decorating it, inflicted years before at a tribal sun-dance ritual.

The gleeful warriors spun Orlo around, began to drag away the mud-daubed, shirtless half-breed.

Suddenly, a surprised cry of "Wait!" rang out. Angry Bear stood saucer-eyed, staring at the whip-marked skin of Orlo Brubaker's back. The severe slash marks he'd received at his flogging had healed into worm-like purplish ridges that laddered all the way from his waist to his shoulder blades.

The sight might have made a white man gag.

But it made Angry Bear and his braves grunt with admiration!

"Poison Snake," said Angry Bear, his voice tinged with awe and envy. "You must have taken part in a powerful ritual to prove yourself brave. I have never seen such a mass of honorable scars! They must be very, very strong medicine."

Orlo didn't dare to appear relieved. "Oh, they *are* right strong medicine, chief."

"It must be so, my brother! My *brave* brother!" The chief's countenance, once menacing, was now friendly. The Blackfoot leader went on, "And you said something about having brought gifts? Something about thunder sticks? And news about some Long Knives ripe for killing and scalping?"

"All those things, and more."

Angry Bear yanked his buffalo lance from the ground before his lodge, pumped it twice above his head. Immediately warriors and squaws began to converge from around the village. "We'll feast on puppy meat and squaw cabbage this night, until our bellies burst, in honor of the band's newest warrior, Poison Snake!''

The chief stood arm-in-arm with the one-time captive. ''In fact, when I look at you now, the more I do seem to recall you. Poison Snake—yes, even the name is coming back!''

''Well, like I said, chief, it's been more than a few summers.''

The chief ushered Orlo into his lodge, his face wreathed in smiles. Soon the pipe with the slobbery mouthpiece was being passed back and forth.

Finally Orlo let himself heave a sigh. Out of the woods, by God!

The half-breed's vengeance bent was thoroughly fueled. Now to get the Blackfeet's blood up and on a killing rampage!

Chapter 21

Under a welcome sunny sky Pike and McConnell rode, moving rapidly across country down pine-stippled mountainsides, over gully-scoured hills, through mazes of coulees, large and not-so-large. Birds watched them from the trees, animals from the ground, wary of the intruders in their domain.

But the determination of the mountain men left no time for hunting. Pike's hunch remained strong: danger lay in the path of Fred and Bright Cloud.

Now the forest fell away, granting a clear view of a verdant valley. "Well, Skins, we made it. Crossed the Divide, and found us the Shoshone lands. But now we've got another problem. Plenty of villages up ahead. One of 'em holds Buffalo Tail's band, but which?"

"Another thing," McConnell added. "We can't be sure that Standing Antelope guessed right. Bright Cloud could've picked a different bunch to join. Or maybe she and Fred never did get this far."

Pike's face was grim, reflecting his mood. "We

137

need to find out, Skins, and find out soon. Even if things went wrong, there could still be time to look for the couple if they're lost. Find out if they're held captive. If so, stage a rescue.''

''Jesus!''

''Skins, we've got to split up. You range southeast and I'll range southwest. Stop at every village, talk to every Shoshone you meet. Ask about Bright Cloud.''

''And her Long Knife boyfriend, don't forget.''

Pike leaned in the saddle, punched McConnell's arm. McConnell didn't wince. ''Say, your arm, it's feeling all well again?''

Skins grinned. ''Like that Blackfoot never clobbered it. Feels fine. Just like your healed scalp wound. And Pike? I didn't really think, just now, that you'd forgotten Fred.''

''I didn't think that you thought I'd forgot.'' Then, he added, ''Agreed then, we'll go separate ways? At the next fork in the trail.''

''Hell, we're *at* the next fork. Look!''

''Be seeing you then, Skins. Ride easy.''

Pike took the upslope trail, McConnell the downslope trail.

They had their tasks cut out for them, and they both knew it.

Chapter 22

"What's that noise?" hissed Bright Cloud as she jumped to her feet beside Fred and scanned the woods around their camp.

Fred joined her, eyes probing the long, late-afternoon shadows. "I don't see anything."

"Neither do I. I heard something, though—or at least, I thought I did. But I don't hear it now."

"Maybe you're just jumpy."

"I'm alert, Fred. It's the way of my people, drummed into us from childhood. To always be on the watch for enemies."

He sat back down on the ground, sober-faced. "Come here to me, honey."

She came.

He drew her down beside him. She frowned and said, "We should have been at the Shoshone village days ago. But we've gone slowly, often taken the long way around."

"Nothing wrong with your idea," Fred said. "To avoid the parties of roaming Blackfeet."

She peered into those blue eyes that she loved. "If any happen to come across us, we're lost, you know."

"Are the Blackfeet so bad?"

"They are very, *very* bad. They don't show the least mercy to their enemies."

Fred leaned back against a tree, pressed his bride-to-be's head to his chest. "Don't you worry, honey. The Leland luck's still holding, I feel it in my bones. And this'll be over soon." There was a moment of tender quiet between them, and then, "Hand me my sketchbook, won't you Bright Cloud? I see a unique spider fern, and I'd like to make a sketch."

Instead, the woman's body tensed. "There it is! That noise again."

"Bright Cloud, you hear a magpie."

"No, it's signals I'm hearing! Warriors' signals! Fred, let's get to our guns!"

The man rolled one way, and the woman leaped the other. Each scooped up a primed flintlock pistol. Should they try to reach their mounts? The horses hobbled in the clearing were nickering in answer to unseen Indian ponies.

A few yards from Fred, there was movement in a thorny sumac clump. A dark face appeared through leafy branches, distorted by a fierce grimace. The shavetail raised his weapon, aimed at the Blackfoot. Then a piercing, ululating cry surprised him from the rear. Leland spun to face a strongly built, wild-eyed warrior who'd leaped from behind an outcropping.

The Blackfoot, raising the war club clenched in his fist, charged.

Meanwhile, Bright Cloud ran to save her man.

When only a few steps away from his assailant, she pointed her gun, triggered and launched a spear of flame. A two-hundred-grain ball slammed into the chest of the warrior and he back-flipped into the creek, dyeing the water with his crimson blood.

Howling now in fury, three more Blackfeet charged into the fray. A bowstring twanged and an arrow zipped, but flew wild. Fred Leland, struggling with a brawny warrior, took a blow to his temple that sent hot a pain bolting through his head. His pistol dropped, and his limp, twitching form followed it to slam the ground.

The woman was struggling in the grip of a strong brave. Her eyes flashed fury, but her arms were pinned.

A heavy quiet filled the small clearing.

What next? thought Bright Cloud.

Then a bolt of cold fear shot through her.

Why, she *did* know what was in store. For Fred and for her!

They'd be put through hell, Blackfeet style!

She bit her lip and glared defiance.

Chapter 23

McConnell reined up his gelding on the deep-tawny rimrock, and scanned the broad, grassy canyon floor that stretched below. Shining in its depths was a winding creek's silver ribbon, and beside it in the distance stood some upright cones. At least a score of Indian lodges, Shoshone in style.

The horse tossed its head and stamped. The mountain man stroked its neck, squinting his eyes in the bright daylight's glare. Yes, he was not only reasonably sure of the tribe, he was now positive.

Shoshones.

The towering Rockies at his back, Skins clicked his mount into motion, began the downslope trot. His cowhide-thonged Hawken, riding his shoulder, felt heavy, for it had been a long day in the saddle.

That day was almost over now.

It was well before sundown when he reached outskirts of the village.

Now that he was close, McConnell counted exactly twenty-two tepees. From the tops, past the elk-skin flaps, protruded slim pine poles, finger-like and aimed at the sky. From among the hide-covered dwellings his arrival was watched by dark-haired, dark-skinned people—men, women, children and curious ponies.

As he rode in, dogs began to prance and bark, but ignoring them he smiled and gigged the blaze-faced bay on. He figured the smile on his face would be viewed as friendly, which it was. According to Pike's advice, he headed for the west end of the village. He knew that in that place of honor he'd undoubtedly find the east-facing lodge of the chief.

Now the rider was surrounded by a small chattering throng, men and women from ancient to young, and plenty of naked children dancing about excitedly. The men weren't hostile in the presence of the white man—but why should they be? The Shoshones were white men's friends, weren't they?

A boy about ten years old touched Skins's leg with a stick, then ran off, gleeful at counting coup.

By now a bent, prune-faced old man had begun to hobble ahead of Skins, waving his arms and intoning in a sing-song voice. This village crier, Skins knew, would have been awarded his position for brave deeds performed in his prime. "Ho! A visitor," he wailed over and over. "A White Eyes guest comes to the village of Walking Spotted Horse!"

McConnell reined in, and the Shoshones formed a ring around him. He knew he was at the chief's lodge by the strung-up medicine bundle of wolf skin and a few black-haired scalps. The buffalo-hide flap was flung back and out stepped a well-built man with copper skin and high cheek bones.

The paint on his chest appeared non-threatening to McConnell. Sure enough, the redskin gave a welcoming smile.

"Greetings, chief," McConnell signed in hand-talk. "I'm called Skins McConnell. Friend of He-Whose-Head-Touches-the-Sky. And how are *you* called?"

The head man's voice croaked gutterally, "No need to sign. I know some of the White Eyes's tongue. I am called Walking Spotted Horse." He put a hand against McConnell's chest.

"Pleased to meet you, Walking Spotted Horse. I've come looking for . . ."

"Wait! First we will smoke the pipe, become friends. Then eat. *Then* talk of why you come." The chief went in his lodge and left McConnell to follow.

The eating part sounded tempting. Skins could smell fresh deer cooking in the encampment's pots.

Inside, Walking Spotted Horse motioned Skins to the guest sitting place at his left. Next the chief brought out his pipe and pouch of smoking blend—a bit of tobacco mixed with crushed willow and aspen leaves. Using a coal from the firepit, Walking Spotted Horse lit the pipe, which was long-stemmed and adorned with feathers. He took a puff and passed it to Skins, who also took a puff.

The red man and the white man smoked in silence, passing the pipe back and forth. Then, "Soon the women of my lodge will bring food. Tell me now, Oh Skins, your reason for coming to this village."

McConnell explained about Bright Cloud, daughter to Standing Antelope, adding a description of the Long Knife who was traveling with the squaw, the

144

one called Fred Leland. McConnell also said a bit about the couple's plans to marry.

Walking Spotted Horse shook his head. "Not see."

"You haven't seen Bright Cloud or Leland?"

"Walking Spotted Horse says what he means. Not see those two, Oh Skins!"

"Does Walking Spotted Horse remember his brother, Standing Antelope?"

"Remembers him, yes. And has seen Bright Cloud too, many times long ago. Only not now for, maybe, seven moons, eight moons."

Shit! McConnell blurted inwardly. "Well then, chief," he added aloud. "I reckon I'll be on my way."

But Walking Spotted Horse kept him from rising. "Sunset comes soon—too late for riding, Oh Skins. You shall eat with me, and my people will give you a place to sleep. There is a lodge near this one, a guest lodge." This time he gave a sly grin.

"You do our band honor by your visit, Oh Skins. I wish to see to it you enjoy the night to come."

His belly full, McConnell lounged atop a pile of pelts. The guest lodge wasn't completely dark. A small, low fire glowed in the tepee's center. The meal of venison and tender plants had satisfied his stomach hunger, which was but one of his hungers.

Now he reckoned it was time for sleep.

But just as he was dozing, there came a scratching at the thick hide wall.

"Christ," he grunted. "Now what?"

Padding to the entrance flap, he drew it back.

In the light from the fire, McConnell's eyes met those of a young Indian woman. "I am called Aspen Leaf. I wish to come in."

She suited action to word, and once she'd ducked inside he saw that he liked her looks. Her doeskin dress hung on a clean-limbed and compact frame, and although she had a typically Shoshone roundish face, her coppery skin had a satin sheen.

"Well," the mountain man said, "if you've come to fetch something, don't mind me."

She smiled, showing pearly teeth.

The girl gracefully went to her knees in front of him, allowing her skirts to climb, revealing plump, brown thighs.

She took his hand in one of hers, and McConnell husked, "You're too kind, Aspen Leaf. Well, go ahead and get what you came for. I confess, I'm getting hot in these damned clothes."

The woman stared, bewildered. Then she opened her dress, showing a dusky breast and nipple.

McConnell hunkered by the fire. The woman, following him, murmured, "Don't you want to lie with me? Or are you the kind who likes other men?"

Skins shook his head. "Well, no. But I wouldn't want to rile Walking Spotted Horse."

Aspen Leaf said, "Don't you understand? I'm a Shoshone chief's gift for you to enjoy this night. I watched you ride in, and saw a strong warrior. Now I claim you."

She whipped her dress over her black-tressed head.

Naked, she showed a vee thatch to match her raven

hair that hung to her breasts. From crown to toe, her skin was coppery brown.

He was climbing out of his duds, too. Laughing, she piped, "You have a big body. A big man's stalk. Now, let Aspen Leaf show you her favorite way to couple."

Before he could whistle "Yankee Doodle," she was on her hands and knees atop the bed of furs. She elevated and wriggled a lush, brown hind end.

McConnell was treated to a view of a set of labia that were swollen with desire. The Shoshone woman's lips burgeoned like plump grapes, and the tab, what could be seen, was as hard as a rifle ball.

So she wanted it doggy-style? Well-l-l . . .

McConnell fingered her pulsing button, as his enormous cockhead nudged her silky folds. A drop of lubricant oozed from his slit. She spread her legs more, parting the soft, slick featherlips.

He leaned over her back, kissed the side of her neck, sighed into her ear. Simultaneously he cleaved her rump with his cock, and speedily sank his full length into her. He started to pump, regularly and slowly, keeping his angle just so, the friction steady.

Her thick, waist-length hair covered her shoulders and hung down. Skins McConnell pistoned again and again, his large balls slapping her paired honey globes.

As he began to feel her spasm inwardly, he spread her cheeks further apart. A smile of happiness curling her lips, desire surging in her blood, her climax grew close. Aspen Leaf braced herself on the bed of furs, heart drumming against her ribs.

McConnell gave a violent thrust and Aspen Leaf shuddered, commenced to come. The man, sensing her time, rammed and rammed her body as the woman met his driving strokes. He was losing his mind, going out of control. "Aah-aah-ee-iii!" she yelped.

She was inviting him to pound as hard as he could. McConnell's breath whistled in his throat, the tension in his balls' sack melting, melting. He could feel the gouts of semen flooding her channel. Her insides quaked and shook. McConnell held her pinned till he was emptied, spent.

The couple flopped down side by side, the man's hard breathing drowned by pleasured sighs.

Somehow Skins didn't think that was all the fun he'd get that night.

She pulled him close to her again—by his cock.

Now Skins *knew* he'd be getting more.

Lots more!

Chapter 24

The leader of the Blackfeet who'd subdued Fred Leland and Bright Cloud, the tallest and strongest of the band, yelped out a exultant cry. Half his surviving warriors, four, dragged the groggy Fred to a stout cottonwood and bound him there.

The others used rough hands to strip off Bright Cloud's clothes, then shoved her, naked and struggling, flat onto her back on the stony earth. Her arms were yanked above her head, and a heavy Blackfoot knelt on each. Two other warriors yanked her legs violently apart, obscene laughter rising in their throats, their snake eyes glittering with cruelty and lust.

Icy dread clawed the woman's heart, but remembering a Shoshone doesn't show fear, she glared defiance at her tormentors. The breechclout of the leader bulged, until he pushed down the grease-grimed width of buckskin. A lascivious grin crossed his coppery face, and he shuffled toward her, penis erect as a hunter's buffalo lance.

He growled something in the Blackfeet tongue. She couldn't understand the words, but got the drift. By now Fox-With-Foot-Missing was playing with his thick cock, getting ready to drop on her. She fought again to get away, but five warriors were too many, and she was helpless.

She said not a word, but her dark eyes flashed hatred. Her abuser grabbed her by the hair, shoved his manhood in her face and scrounged it around. He pressed the leaking tip into her eye, then dragged it downward across her breasts and belly. Sickened to the core, she heard the brute laughing.

The savage rapist knelt between her thighs, plunged brutally.

"Aaa-eeii!" Bright Cloud couldn't help but cry. Fox-With-Foot-Missing's shaft punished her pain-seared channel. She flung her head about on her slim neck, but couldn't escape. The core at the joining of her thighs flamed like fire, and from that point pain spread to fill her body. The rapist's fingers tracked her breasts, and as he pumped relentlessly he bruised her elsewhere. Her tender love cleft was turned to mashed flesh by his hammer.

Then he gushed his wad and flung from the woman, only to be replaced in the saddle by another brute. Bright Cloud's tender juncture was punished by a second onslaught, as rough as the first and equally humiliating.

"Ohh! Dear God!" she thought she heard, and opening her eyes, she saw Fred Leland, bound and staring. The shavetail had revived, and was being forced to witness the suffering of his loved one.

"Bright Cloud . . . Bright Cloud!" Fred groaned. She tried to lift her bottom, but was was thrust back. She attempted other moves, but was punched in the midriff, then rammed harder by the cock that happened to impale her at the moment.

All eight of the braves took their turns, falling upon and toying with her, prying open her mouth, pinching her nipples. They rolled her onto her stomach, and she felt her anus violated as by a white-hot poker. This was the worst pain yet, and it went on and on. Blinded by her agonies, she heard the rutting men's loud grunts.

When they finished their first turns, would each of the Blackfeet take seconds? Or would they kill her, which could only mean relief? Finally the last brave's organ dwindled and he withdrew and rolled off. She readied herself for the killing war-club blow.

It didn't come.

She opened her eyes.

Gabbling chatter filled the clearing, and approaching hooves shuffled near. Ponies were being brought up. The woman saw Fred thrown across a mare's back and tied. She felt her aching self flung aboard a pinto, rawhide thongs digging her neck, wrists and ankles.

Fred, in his days with the troop, had done some listening to the enlisted men. The tales of Blackfeet torture had made his blood run cold. Now, if his captors weren't going to kill him on the spot, they must be taking him to their village.

Jesus! Jesus God!

Bright Cloud had suffered, and his turn was next.

151

Fox-With-Foot-Missing gave an exultant cry, and the ponies moved out.

Torture in the Blackfeet village?

Jesus God! Jesus God!

Chapter 25

The Indian village Pike came to was situated on a meadow fronting a wide but very shallow river. Urging his gelding down the bank, he held his rifle and horns at arm's length overhead, and although the splashing of the horse wet his buckskins, his powder stayed dry.

In another dozen yards he was riding among the bunched lodges. The village crier, as usual, put in an appearance. "A visitor, a visitor!" came the to-be-expected call.

Bronze-skinned old Buffalo Tail stood in front of a large tepee. The chief was grayer than the last time Pike had seen him, and his spine bent under the load of his more-than-sixty winters. His cragged, parchment-skinned face smiled at the sight of the mountain man.

"He-Whose-Head-Touches-the-Sky," he croaked in Shoshone. "We have not seen each other in two summers."

"More like three."

Pike dismounted amid the friendly crowd that had gathered, nodding greeting at several warriors of his acquaintance. The chief shambled up to press his hand to Jack Pike's chest. Pike returned the gesture, and then stepped back.

"It is good to see you again, He-Whose-Head-Touches-the-Sky. You come for a reason?"

"Oh Chief Buffalo Tail, there's something I would speak of."

"First we'll have a feast!"

"Sounds good, chief. Damned good."

Pike let brown boys tussle for the privilege of walking his horse down to water. Eventually Buffalo Tail took him inside the lodge, and a stone-bowled, feather-festooned pipe materialized. Soon the pipe was reeking streams of pungent smoke, the Indian inhaling, then passing the piece to Pike. The men had hardly finished the ceremony when the chief's wives started passing bowls of boiled venison and skunk cabbage.

Pike pitched in and found the eating good. When the meal had ended, and Pike rubbed his belly to express satisfaction, he asked if Fred Leland and Bright Cloud had been seen in the village.

"This Bright Cloud, she is known to Buffalo Tail," the chief said. "Well known. But the woman has not been here for many moons. I must tell you, He-Whose-Head-Touches-the-Sky, it is a good thing the girl has found a man she'll accept for a husband."

"Well, I'm sure you'll welcome the couple if they make their way here."

The old man nodded. "It would be a good marriage celebration. The women of the village will bring dresses, leggings, bracelets and fine new moccasins, and a new lodge will be set up for the couple. That is, when and *if* Bright Cloud and the white man she's chosen come. Remember, He-Whose-Head-Touches-the-Sky, to reach this place they must pass through Blackfeet country. The couple could be in danger now.''

Pike grunted agreement. "Buffalo Tail, your mind runs along the same lines as mine. That's why, come tomorrow, I'll be riding out to look for Bright Cloud and Fred. Maybe I'll run into 'em, maybe I won't.''

Buffalo Tail smiled. "I am glad that you saw fit to visit this village, my brother. Of course, you'll sleep this night in the visitor's lodge.''

"Thanks, chief,'' the mountain man said.

Pike sat on the bed of furs in the roomy village guest lodge. It was after dark and he was preparing for sleep, but now he heard a scratching at the outside of the hide wall.

He thought he knew what he was hearing. He smiled in the light of the low-burning tepee fire. Sure enough, it was as he expected, and the entrance flap was drawn back. A womanly shape stepped inside to join him. "Well, lady, you're as welcome as . . .''

What cut the mountain man's words off was the entrance of a second delightful female! Both the Indian maidens were clad in doeskin dresses, both were young and attractive in an Indian sort of way. The Shoshone girls stepped close and smiled shyly at Pike.

He was looking them over in the flickering firelight when they both began disrobing. Down came the raven hair and off came the dresses.

"Well, gals, old Buffalo Tail, he sure does know how to treat a fella well."

A young, seductive woman placed herself on either side of Pike, hips swelling in tawny splendor, dusky globular breasts ripe, dollar-sized areolas bullet-hard and puckering. The cylinder of flesh between Pike's legs grew rigid, its pulsations radiating heat through his massive frame. The woman on his right sank to her pretty knees, and the mountain man could see her thighs, tawny and very smooth.

She took one of his hands and placed it on a bare breast, looking up at him in appeal. But it was the other woman who conquered her shyness first, saying, "You are the visiting warrior who is called He-Whose-Head-Touches-the-Sky. I am called Flower Petal. This other girl is my sister, and she is called Gentle Stream."

"Flower Petal and Gentle Stream?"

"Yes, Oh He-Whose-Head-Touches-the-Sky."

"And I gather that you're here with Buffalo Tail's permission?"

Gentle Stream piped up with a sweet, bell-clear voice, "Permission? Yes. That is, the chief doesn't object to our coming. But the decision was ours, He-Whose-Head-Touches-the-Sky. When you rode into the village we watched, then ran swiftly to the headman to tell him our wish. We wanted to be the ones to offer ourselves as hospitality toward the chief's guest. Of course, your beautiful body made us eager to share you."

"Two women, and not one. Hmm. Well, what'll be your pleasure, gals? You want to take turns?"

Two smiles now, and much less shy. "If turns are taken, one girl must go first. This would be difficult for a Shoshone, all of whom consider themselves equal. How to decide, He-Whose-Head-Touches-the-Sky?"

Pike stood stroking his beard. His pecker was stretching his britches like a circus tent, but he continued stroking his beard. "Well, if choosing one over the other is gonna cause hard feelings—if you'll pardon the expression."

"Hard," Flower Petal giggled.

"Feeling!" Gentle Stream pealed a laugh.

Then both the Shoshone women were over Pike like sweat-lodge smoke. The finger-combing of his hair was mind-blowing, but the caresses of his cock inflamed Pike to his soul.

The next thing he knew, Gentle Stream was gluing her soft-furred pelvis against his. "Front or rear, you don't care?" he rasped. "Fine with me! Well, there'll be time for both ways, I allow." Then he settled back and let things take their course.

The women reached out at the same time, and formed a cooperative team for hauling down Pike's britches. The mountain man's turgid, thick member sprang free. "Oh, so big!" cried wide-eyed Flower Petal.

Gentle Stream, like her sister, registered happy surprise. Now Flower Petal was peeling the shirt from

Pike's sinewy upper body. At the same time she maneuvered him, sweating, toward a pile of furs spread on the packed-earth floor.

Gentle Stream plastered her body to Pike's, and the panting couple sank onto a dense, soft buffalo robe. As the mountain man lay on his back, the woman threw a leg across him and promptly lowered herself. Next, with Flower Petal's eager aid, Gentle Stream clasped and guided Pike's urgent pole. With a sigh, the lithe, strong gal impaled herself, her velvet portal parting to swallow the big man's throbbing phallus.

With her honey-slit slick with juice, Pike bottomed his flesh–spear delightfully.

As the woman's inner contractions pulsed wildly, her spidering hands roamed the mountain man's nakedness. The ample bosom flattened against his chest, and he squirmed his hips to skewer her still more deeply. Close by his side, Flower Petal gave a mew, cat-like, and with eager touch stroked his member.

The sensation sent Pike into a pleasant frenzy. Gentle Stream, catching the spirit, bucked and heaved under him. His noble staff brought her, shuddering, to a climax.

Now the white man and two Indian women huddled together, still with arms and legs entwined. But no sooner did Jack Pike's overheated body start to cool than he felt exquisite sensations pulling him back from quietude.

Ah, those eager, questing hands bringing his cock back to full arousal!

Flower Petal's fondling brought him all the way back, and twisting their bodies and swapping ends, the threesome again sprawled happily all over each other. Now it was Flower Petal who rode the mountain man, the twitching of his mast synchronized with her tunnel's spasmings. Trying to go her sister one better, Gentle Stream glued her ass crack to Pike's chest, at the same time she leaned her face toward the coupled crotches. Soon her lips and tongue were teasing Flower Petal's love fronds, which were spread wide by the mountain man's wonder wand.

Flower Petal climaxed with a loud groan, but didn't stop there, so ecstatic was her heat. She began bouncing up and down, buttocks pounding Pike's pelvis around his engulfed endowment. At the satiny touch of her sister's mouth, she and the man lapsed into mindless thrashing. With Gentle Stream's fingers on his fattened scrotal sack, Pike found himself gushing and gushing some more. Mellow grunts from the woman under him accompanied her flooding.

Quaking with delight, Flower Petal, too, spun into heaven. The moments stood still for the blissful threesome. Basking in afterglow, they lay side by side, panting.

And yet, somehow, Pike knew he wasn't yet through for the night.

Less than an hour later the women were at him again. He rose to the occasion, and soon had them gushing, squealing.

Chapter 26

It was almost noon of the bright, blue-skied day as Pike rode his bay out on the apex of the high-trail mountain overlook. The sun was hot on the Norway pine-clad slopes, but the mountain man wasn't enjoying the wild beauty of the scene. Instead, his attention was drawn to the valley below, where there rolled along, of all things, a mule-drawn covered wagon!

Here, hundreds of miles off the main-traveled Oregon route, deep in Blackfeet country?

Merely one of the cumbersome "rolling lodges," not even an attempt by the wagoners to achieve safety in numbers?

Jesus! Are the pilgrims half-wits?

Pike gigged the horse off the promontory and downslope. He'd have words with the wagoners, of course, in the manner of all whites encountering each other in this wilderness. There might even be news of Fred and Bright Cloud, although Pike doubted it. His latest hunch was that the couple hadn't made it this far.

Since leaving Buffalo Tail's stronghold, the big mountain man had checked four other Shoshone villages. He'd acquired no positive information at any, only garnered welcomes and hospitality—loads of hospitality! Now he rode with a semi-numb, whacked-out cock flaccid against his saddle leather. He was trailing again, but this time back north, still keeping his eyes peeled for the sought-for couple.

But with less chance, as more days passed, of finding Fred and Bright Cloud alive and safe.

He knew the mountains had their way of concealing secrets—some of them pleasant surprises, some of them ghastly ones. But as long as there was hope, he'd be damned if he gave up the search.

Suddenly, below him on the flat, there was movement. Alarming movement!

Down where the wheels' dust rose in saffron rooster combs, a number of horsemen galloped out from behind a monolith.

Blackfeet! A small war party.

Shots rang out. Some of the shots came from guns wielded by redskins!

Recalling the theft of army guns by Orlo Brubaker, Pike was hardly surprised. Something like this was bound to happen. The big man gave a quick check to his own guns' priming, then, Hawken held at the ready, put his mount into a downhill lope.

Below, Jacobus Raleigh, immigrant, whipped up his four-span team, and the mules heedlessly ran like hell. ''Shoot th' infernal Injuns!'' yelled the sodbuster. "Hey, kin o' mine, back in the wagon box, kill all red devils ya can!"

Back in the lurching rear of the wagon a woman and teenager knelt, unlimbering their shooting-irons. In the cloth bonnet's pucker-hole, there was room for both would-be marksmen.

Son Rob's musket and wife Agatha's fowling piece belched. Flame, smoke and pellets flew.

Not a single Indian pitched from his pony's back. Instead, a hail of arrows struck the sides of the wagon, sticking there.

"Whillikers, maw, we missed."

"Keep down, son, and reload! We're from the Arkansas Ozarks, and plenty tough. That's why yer paw brung us on this shortcut to th' Oregon lands."

Fifteen warriors—the whole war party led by Iron Kettle—swept in a wide half-circle behind the jouncing wagon, gaining as they raced. All the Indians rode war-painted ponies, were hideously and brightly painted themselves. All whooped horrendously, since they meant business, killing business. On either side of the leather-lunged subchief rode the bloodthirsty braves, Long Jaw and Flattened Nose.

Flattened Nose, riding at full gallop, thumbed back the hammer on his unfamiliar musket, let off a shot that broke the back of the Raleighs' lead mule. The creature went down screaming, tangled harness tripping the others animals of the team.

As this went on, the warrior riding beside Long Jaw flung up his hands, jolted by a slug. His painted chest fountaining gore, he pitched from his mount, eyes glazed and sightless. He hit the ground head-

first, and was trampled to mincemeat [...]
following.

Now the wagon halted, vulnerable on the flat. The mules, in their tangled traces bucked, brayed and lashed out, kicking. From under the canvas the Raleigh family fired, reloaded and fired again. Flights of feathered shafts rained on their vehicle, a few flint arrowheads piercing settler flesh.

Old Raleigh sustained a forearm wound and blood flowed freely. The younker's ear dangled from a skin flap, while his mother, furious, shot a warrior, bursting his groin to shreds.

The members of the band, responding to a shout from their leader, surrounded the wagon. Galloping in a ring, they fired from under their ponies' necks. Thus the redskin riders were hard to kill, while a constant arrow-fall reached the wagon, pincushioning it.

Into the midst of the chaos galloped Jack Pike, the gray gelding under him surging allout. The mountain man raised his Hawken. The weapon bucked, spat fire and lead. The painted face of Crazy Loon dissolved in a crimson mist, as brain–matter and bone–shards burst from the rear of his skull.

In the wagon, young Rob cried, ''Maw! Looks like help wearin' a beard and buckskins!''

The sight of yelping warriors and the whiz of arrows had terrified the woman. Speechlessly she hugged her son, as blood from his injured ear soaked

...board Jacobus fired another ... short and did no damage.

...ring his Kentucky pistol at the ... the snorting nose of a pony explode, ...der catapulting from its back. That ri- ...ance flew skyward, flexing as it dropped. It ...d point-first in the ground, and as he swept past, Pike managed to snag it. Then, wheeling the gray, he kicked his heels and drove the mount straight at a similarly armed enemy.

Rope-muscled Long Jaw galloped toward the mountain man, his own stout lance leveled for spearing. But at the last minute Pike bent low, hugging the bay's neck and avoiding the fatal blow.

Meanwhile the lance he used impaled the redskin warrior, driving into his abdomen and coming out his back. Mangled intestines sprang from both openings, the slithering coils unwinding in the air, flogging nearby warriors and blinding them with blood-spray.

From the wagon of the whites crackled another light volley, and two more Blackfeet were punched from ponies, flopping to earth where they lay blood-drenched, motionless. Unhorsed Indians flopped on the ground like trout, while the rampaging mountain man, who'd lost the lance, unsheathed his tomahawk.

"Outa the wagon, Rob! Let's help the fella."

So saying, Jacobus put bootsoles to dirt, and together with his offspring waded in armed with lumber axes. Most of the Blackfeet had used up their gun-powder and were eager to be dueling with blades again. Leaping from their mounts and yelling savagely, they ran at the whites.

One of those shouting throats was ruined by Mrs. Raleigh's shotgun blast, the voice box of the warrior exploding and showering gristle bits.

"Ha-ya-*yee*EE!" whooped Rutting Bull, bounding to his death. He met Pike head on as the mountain man leaned from horse, tomahawk slicing. At the same instant he brained the squat red man, Rob Raleigh cut the legs—literally—from a brave called Tall Oak.

The double-amputee stared with disbelief, then toppled, paint on his face mingling with pooled blood from his stumps.

By now Pike was engaged with the subchief, both men armed with knives, circling . . . circling. Other combatants' action boiled around these two, but both men knew the outcome of the battle would be decided here and now. Both were fighters born and fighters bred, and both had warrior instincts finely honed. Each respected what the other meant to do—which was kill, by fair means or foul.

Pike gazed into the broad, high-cheekboned face, rendered horrific with bold vermilion stripes.

The battlers closed in, Pike feinting with his blade. The subchief lashed out in return. Metal flashed and clashed.

The warrior moved strongly, lightning-like. The mountain man's Green River spun from his grip.

Damn, the Blackfoot was good—that one time!

Pike stood rooted to earth, arms outstretched. Opening his mouth wide, he gave a shout, "Chief, look behind you! By God, it's the White Eyes axman!"

The split-second's distraction was all he needed. Pike grabbed the warrior, wrenched him from his feet, limbs flailing. He flung bold Iron Kettle into a sharp-cornered boulder, and heard the spine give with a crisp *snap!*

Suddenly, the other Blackfeet froze in their tracks, their expressions horrified.

"Git, you bastards!" Jack Pike roared out. "Git, I say!" It was almost comical, the Blackfeet rushing to their horses. *Almost* comical.

Within minutes they'd gone, even carrying off their dead and wounded.

The mountain man and the immigrant faced each other. Both were sweaty, tired of arm and smeared with blood, but they could grin, and did. "Sometimes it happens that way," Pike explained to the man. "Kill the chief, and the not-so-braves cry, 'Bad medicine.' By the way, Pike's my name. Jack Pike."

"Jacobus Raleigh, from the neighborhood of Fort Smith. This here's m'son Rob. Wife's in the wagon." Forgetting entirely to mention thanks, he grumbled, "One span of mules still alive, Pike. Reckon we can cobble harness for 'em?"

"Wouldn't doubt it."

From the wagon, "Jacobus? Who's that with ya? Did the dang fool draw the Injuns our way?"

"By the way, pilgrim," Pike said casually. "On

your travels did you happen to see a white man with an Indian gal? He'd be in his mid-twenties, and wearing army blue. And the Shoshone gal's pretty as a rose of summer.''

Chapter 27

When Fred Leland and Bright Cloud were led into the village of Angry Bear's band, tied belly down across hunting ponies, they were jeered and tumbled to the ground roughly enough to raise huge dust puffs. Next the captives were punched, stoned and kicked, in the case of the Shoshone, the blows falling on bare flesh. Then one of the warrior societies decided Fred, too, should be dragged around stark naked.

Words were barked at the smooth-faced officer, who couldn't understand a word of the Blackfeet tongue. Then his ears were boxed, his nose pinched, eye sockets gouged—all painfully. Then finally, into his tear-dimmed view strode a figure he could recognize.

Fred was not the least bit glad to see the deserter from the army's ranks.

"Private Brubaker! You? Here?"

"Well, well, leftenant," said the breechclout-clad, vicious half-breed. "A wrong thing, your callin' me 'private.' I ain't in the U.S. Army no more! And neither are you, ain't that right?'' His ugly face split in a malicious grin. ''Sorry by now that you wouldn't pay me blackmail? If not, you will be.''

Leland nodded in the direction of the arm-tied Bright Cloud. ''If you mean we might be tortured, she and me . . .''

''You're wrong about that, shavetail.''

Hope surged in the young man. Was his luck due to come back, at least somewhat? ''Wrong that we'll be tortured?''

A sneering laugh. ''On, no. Wrong that it's a 'might' thing. No 'might,' about it, Leland Pipsqueak! You'll be tortured all right, and there'll be no mercy. Startin' soon now!''

Leland's impassioned voice shook. ''A man who'd desert, run off to join an Indian band, make war . . .''

''Worse than a fella as'd desert, run off to an Indian band, so's to dip his wick in a slut squaw?''

''Brubaker, you bastard!''

Orlo leveled a kick at Fred's unprotected come-together, which collapsed Fred to the ground, to puke and writhe.

''What next?'' asked big, strong Stinging Hornet, a violence-prone subchief.

''Strip the captive and tie him to a tree. For a real torture party we got to wait till Angry Bear gets back from the raid he went on.''

''You say well, my brother, Poison Snake. What about her, then?'' He cocked his thumb at Bright Cloud. The woman's eyes shot bolts of wrath and hatred. Her fighting spirit wasn't dead yet.

"Bruised up, ain't she? But she's still a pretty piece of tail."

"True, my brother. True." Stinging Hornet grinned. So did another lustful warrior, Stone Hand, and of course Fox-With-Foot-Missing, who'd already roughly battered her channel with his greased pole several times.

Orlo chuckled obscenely. "How 'bout me first, then you, Stinging Hornet, then the others?"

"Sounds good to me, my brother."

Orlo toed Fred in his cracked ribs. "As for leftenant, whose luck's plumb run out, when he's nekkid, tie him so's he'll have to watch us ream his woman."

Fred knew something horrible was about to happen, and it did. The Blackfeet were ingenious, both the men and women, in their way.

Leland was surrounded by punching, gouging women, stripped totally bare-assed and shoved in a sitting posture, back pressed to the trunk of a dead, leafless cottonwood. Two minutes later he was trussed arms and torso to the tree, legs extended in front of him on the ground. Wet rawhide wrappings confined his wrists, ankles and private parts. Under the hot sun on the unshaded canyon floor, Fred Leland came to feel fear. As uncured rawhide dried, it shrank. A Black-Irishman quartermaster has taught him as much, back at Fort Union. It had been one of the first lessons he'd learned on arriving in the West!

The squeezing of his testicles started to bring pain quickly.

A few yards away, Orlo Brubaker shook his huge, hairy penis.

"I'm gonna screw your squaw till her cunt's raw and bloody, leftenant! I do like to treat women's parts rough. And after me'll come my red brothers! Then all of us'll settle in to wait, maybe for one day, maybe two days. Can't do the two of you to death without our chief bein' here. Angry Bear, he's off on the warpath just now. It gave the chief a real charge, when I presented him with the gov'ment muskets I stole."

"You know something, Brubaker? You're scum!"

"You're worse'n scum, shavetail. You rich Eastern bastards are lousy pimples on the world's ass! That's why my kinda revenge is as sweet as it is." When Brubaker was done with the insults, he sashayed over to the bound Shoshone woman.

Very, very soon the air was rent by screams. Fred was forced to listen—and watch—the ordeal of Bright Cloud as it went on, and on, and on.

When the woman finally passed out, purple dusk had come to the canyon floor. With the onset of the long night, voracious insects swarmed over the helpless victims.

Chapter 28

Captain Maynard Leland dismounted and stood beside his thoroughbred bay with white stockings, under a pine atop a promontory facing the western mountain prospect. Strung out behind the officer were his exploration party, consisting of the troopers and the scientists, plus Standing Antelope's Shoshone scouts. All swung from their saddles to rest and await a decision by their commander.

Leland aimed to give them that decision, any minute now. He raised his field glasses to his steely eyes and played the powerful lenses along that awesome western horizon.

Along the mountains' cresting summits, he knew, lay the Great Divide that spanned the length of the North American continent. It represented the main obstacle to east-west wagon travel, the one he'd been sent out from Fort Union to make a start at dealing with. The land-hungry Easterners, by the thousands, who'd raised their outcry were an impatient lot, and Leland felt the pressure to find newf routes, not only to Oregon but to California and the Utah lands.

New maps would show the the low passes, the passes with the easy grades—the *best* passes. Today Leland felt a good deal of responsibility weighing on his shoulders.

Military duty was his god, and as he'd done throughout his career, he'd put it first, ahead of personal matters. But now, as never before, concern for his only son nagged his weary brain. Would Pike and McConnell be able to find Fred out in the wilderness? Could the mountain men's efforts result in a reunion between father and son?

Had too much time passed?

Weren't the Blackfeet being stirred up by a certain deserter?

Damn Brubaker, the half-breed! the captain thought.

Damn all Indians, including sexy, pretty Bright Cloud!

Leland jammed the field glasses in their case, pulled on his gauntlets and took up his reins. But as he was preparing to mount, a figure in buckskins cantered up. The captain's expression turned sour.

"Yo, cap'n!" sang out Muley Ballou.

Leland growled an order, "Ride back and pass the word, Ballou. I intend to push due west toward that vee notch over there, under that snowcapped peak."

"Jesus, cap'n, that's a powerful waste of your time and my energy! Around Mount Pinyon? Hell, the grade's too steep. Oughtta set your sights yonder, down thataway."

"Toward the south? Man, are you mad? Why Dix and I have estimated altitudes."

"Over Moose Horn Saddle yonder? Sure, the pass, it's low, but too damned steep for wheels and teams! I tell you, cap'n . . ."

He said no more.

A sudden flurry of gunshots rang out, a ragged fusillade!

Over a ridge swept a pounding Blackfeet horde, paint-daubed ponies at the run, the high-country air filled with chilling war cries.

"Sergeant O'Dell!" Leland shouted.. "Never mind bugle calls. Form up the men!"

"Yessir."

And as the next few minutes flew, the war ponies sped, hooves ripping divots from the stony ground and hurling them. Loud banshee howls burst from scores of lungs, as the warriors rode down on the surprised scientific party.

"Mount up, men! Mount up and fire at will! Charge!"

Muskets boomed, spewing powder smoke and lead. Two Blackfeet pitched off their horses, one with blood spurting from his side. The other received a nasty exit wound, where a fifty-caliber ball had torn through his shoulder.

An arrow zipped between the officer and the non-com, the men digging spurs to horses' flanks, jumping their horse to the left and right. Then began the close-quarters charge, heavy, strong-haunched cavalry mounts surging into motion. As iron-shod hooves clattered and stones flew, sabers glittered in the morning light. Muley Ballou hung back, but the troopers stood in their stirrups, eager to go after the enemy, eager to defeat them.

Screams of agony were raised on both sides, as terrible wounds were dealt to living flesh. Figures clad in blue engaged braves daubed with hideous war paint, men pitching from horses left and right, bleeding from heads and chests, intestines dragging from ripped abdomens.

Corporal Stanislaus Kowalski howled a sharp cry, throwing his hands to his blown-out cheek and falling. Private Mel Crank felt an arrow sting his buttock. He jerked out the shaft and rode on, straight at a subchief. But another arrow drove through his throat and Crank died, his Tennessee nose plowing Wyoming mountain soil.

"Fall back. Take cover. We're outnumbered!" Then O'Dell, his heart shredded by a slug, slipped from the saddle, dead before he hit the ground. Maynard Leland cursed and waved his saber, thinking, God, what a battle! No company flag, no guidon pennants! And the kill-crazy savages rode skillfully and fought hard. The officer leaped from his plunging mount, and made a dash for the trooper's hole-up place.

Dust billowed up to obscure Leland's vision, and that of the troopers who'd been forced to retreat to the handy rock jumble. On all sides the scared troopers called out to each other.

"The red heathens, they're gettin' set to rush us!"

"Holy Toledo!"

"Christ, corporal, don't I *wish* I was back in Toledo!"

The ground glistened crimson with spilled blood, Leland saw, and the spot where he crouched was surrounded by huddled forms. More than half the defenders were wounded, most of them seriously. The bodies of the dead sprawled all around, and there was a temptation to hoist a white flag, ask for terms.

Then Maynard Leland remembered those were Blackfeet out there.

"Here they come again, cap'n!"

"Bayonets, men! Up and charge 'em! We can beat the red devils yet."

He was on his feet now, still looking dashing, despite the torn and bloodstained uniform. His blond mustache twitched as he raised his sword. He watched the yelling, rampaging Blackfeet hurdle the barrier, started forward on shaky legs, but tripped over the corpse of Melchior Dix. Along the line of soldiers being scythed down by tomahawks, he saw lieutenant Meester take a neck-breaking war club blow.

Then an arrow grazed the captain's temple, and he felt himself passing out, hurtling headfirst through an inky void.

Then Maynard Leland, scion of the socially elite New York Lelands, knew no more for a time.

Chapter 29

In a dark, chilly, fireless camp set low on a slope in the Needle Rock Range, Jack Pike suddenly stiffened where he hunkered, his animal-like senses—those never-failing survival tools—brought him alert to someone approaching.

It was just three days since the battle for the settler's wagon. Neither Jacobus Raleigh nor his family had seen Fred Leland, and so Pike had trailed it back toward the northeast, into the heart of Blackfeet country and this meeting place.

Perhaps the person approaching now was a friend, perhaps an enemy, but whichever, the blood coursed faster in Pike's veins. Scarcely moving his massive bulk, he quietly stretched out his hand to scoop up his Hawken.

Less than an hour ago this early evening, he'd reprimed the weapon.

Now he rolled to his feet and on silent moccasins ghosted to the woods behind the camp. A minute later there came a crackling of bushes and a squishy *clunk,* the stamp of a horse, a horse wearing an iron horse-shoe!

"Jack?" Skins McConnell called. "Are you around, Jack? I see your bedroll. Looks like you got to our rendezvous first." The smaller mountain man turned, scanning the site. "C'mon out! Tell me you found the couple."

Pike stepped from cover. "Skins, you may as well know straight off. I sure haven't found Fred and Bright Cloud. But *you* do look fit! Those Shoshone hospitality gals been treating you right?"

The friends pretended to box for a few seconds, then lowered their arms. "Have you filled your belly?" Pike asked.

"Downed some pemmican on the trail, a bit of parched corn."

"Man, find yourself a stump and set. I'm serving beef jerky, lightly salted."

"*Lightly* salted?"

Pike shrugged. "All right. Salty as hell. The process keeps the meat from ripening. By the way, what kind of luck did you have, seeking Leland and his woman?"

"No luck along that line. And that reminds me, I left something back in the trees. Permission to go fetch it?"

"Sounds like we'll need light to see by. I'll have a fire going, time you get back."

McConnell strode away, but returned shortly. He led two horses, his own and an unshod pony. And besides the animals, he prodded along an Indian boy.

178

The kid looked scared, probably because his hands were tied behind his back.

"Blackfoot?" Pike observed.

"By his moccasins and the raggedy coup feathers, yeah. I found him a mile or so from here, Jack. He tried to get away, but ol' Skins outfoxed him."

Pike grinned in the firelight. He was nursing the blaze, feeding it punk and sticks, and he looked red-faced in the flames. "Nice work, Skins. He could be damned helpful. Shove him this way!"

McConnell obliged.

"I warn you, kid," Pike cautioned. "When I start my questioning, you'd best speak up." The Blackfeet language rolled badly off Pike's palate, but the youth seemed to savvy what he'd heard.

"I'm going to describe a man and woman. He's a White Eyes and she's a Shoshone. About so-o-o tall . . ." A description followed, amplified by hand signals. The kid stared insolently at first, then turned downright sullen.

"Say, kid, how are you called?"

"I am called Stone Badger. The name came from my village's dreaming shaman."

"And how is your chief of your village called?"

"Angry Bear!" He bit it out.

"Now, Stone Badger, here's what I've been getting at. Have you seen the couple I told you about? The White Eyes and the Shoshone?

The kid's jaw clamped, and he said not a word.

"Nothing to say?"

The kid spat in the dirt.

Pike clubbed his knife haft, and boxed young Stone

Badger's left ear. The ear flattened against the kid's head, and when it sprang back it was reddened and stinging. *Very* reddened and stinging. "Kid," the big man snapped, "I aim to have my answers, even if it means handing you a real bad time. There's lives at stake. Lives of folks I'm being paid to save!"

The young Blackfoot's expression was defiant. "You have a White Eyes kind of courage," he spat at Pike, "which really means *no* courage! You have your weapons, and you're willing to use them. *My* hands are empty and tied behind me!"

Pike eyed McConnell. "Y'know, Skins, I'm tired as hell of this. Toss a few more sticks on the fire, will you? Maybe we can heat things up for the kid, get him to tell us things he doesn't want to."

Pike yanked the breechclout from the young Blackfoot, then swiftly hooked a leg around his shin, tripping him and dropped him. From the ground Stone Badger launched a kick, but it was ineffectual. The mountain man grabbed the kid and wrestled him over to the fire. "Now let's you and me have that little chat! Skins, you got that gun barrel plenty hot?"

"Red hot, not white hot."

"Hot enough. I'll hold him, while you press the muzzle to his cock!"

Stone Badger wormed and squirmed. Pike's grip held on his neck and crotch. McConnell brought the Hawken's muzzle close to the kid's come-together.

He lowered the muzzle toward the limp and shriveled target.

"No! No!" The kid bumped and bucked. "Aaa-iieee! You can't do this! You can't! All right, White Eyes! I'll tell you! I'll tell you!''

"Tell us what?''

"About the Long Knife and the Shoshone bitch! How the warriors of my chief's band are holding them.''

"Shoshone *bitch?*''

"That's what Poison Snake calls her.''

"Who's Poison Snake? Oh, never mind. The couple, they're alive?''

The boy's copper face contorted. "Alive for now. Not much longer.''

"Skins, hand me that rifle. Yeah, the hot one.''

"All right! All right! I'll tell!''

Then it all came spilling out, all about Angry Bear's village and how far it was from here to there. Trails. Landmarks. The canyon site and the approaches to it.

"So, all-in-all, from here it's less than a day's ride?''

The Indian kid glared sullenly. Nodded.

"Let him up, Skins. I really can't see killing him. Maybe break his leg, or better, both legs.''

"Put out an eye?''

"Or, better, both eyes. Or how's this, make him half a man? Take off one of the kid's ears, one of his hands, one of his nuts?''

The kid exploded from the ground, breaking from Pike's loosened grip. He powered into a bare-assed sprint, pumping skinny, bowed legs for all he was worth. In a few seconds he was in among the trees, branches crashing as he bulled on through.

McConnell raised a quizzical eyebrow. "Getting soft, Jack? I mean, after all, he's a Blackfoot."

A shrug. "A Blackfoot *kid.*"

"I caught the wink you tossed me. That gun barrel wasn't the least bit hot."

"Well, it'd be hard on the Hawken, sticking one end in a fire. Best to keep the temper of the iron sound. The gun shoots just fine, and I'd like to keep it that way."

McConnell strolled to his horse and stripped off the saddle. Then threw down his bedroll and started to spread his soogans, saying, "I reckon Stone Badger, he'll hightail straight for his village."

"We'll beat him there by days. He's on foot, and we've got horses."

"Do we leave at sunup, then?"

"Better still, be in the saddle by false dawn."

Well down along the mountain trail, Stone Badger was still running pell-mell. When he came to a cliffside with a narrow rock shelf, he kept right on pumping his legs. Although a Blackfoot wasn't supposed to panic, he's done exactly that back there. It had been hell! The giant White Eyes had almost ruined the young brave's manhood.

Now the kid's heart hammered and his lungs heaved, but he still kept running. Sweat flowed into his eyes, half-blinding him. And as if it weren't hard enough to see already, the moon went behind a cloud.

The misstep in the night darkness, was almost inevitable. It happened above a deep, vertical-walled chasm. The shelf crumbled under Stone Badger's moccasin, and the kid went off into thin air, arms pinwheeling. Down he hurtled in spiraling free-fall toward the gorge bottom. Down . . . down . . . down . . .

A big barred owl sailed past on muffled wings.

The mouse in its talons would soon be ripped to shreds, devoured.

Chapter 30

A shaft of morning sunlight beamed in through the smoke hole of the lodge and Fred Leland, tied hand and foot, roused himself from the most troubled sleep he'd experienced in his twenty-six years.

He'd dreamed of demons tearing his body with red-hot pincers, of his being thrown into a vat of boiling brimstone, of seeing his own head being carried on a platter, served to a gigantic painted warrior as tall as a bluff above the Hudson. There'd been a lot of screaming in the nightmare, which now, upon waking, reminded him of Bright Cloud's screams last night.

Now alone in the lodge, he could no longer hear her screams, or for that matter, anyone's. Maybe the woman he loved had been raped to death. Or maybe she'd survived the terrible humiliation, the pain, and was still alive, but was being held on the far side of the Blackfeet village.

After untying him from the tree and dragging him into this lodge, one of his captors had freed his scrotum of its rawhide wrap. Now Fred lay in the tepee, buck-naked, aching from the kicks and blows administered by Orlo Brubaker. Fred had learned the Blackfeet were as vicious and cruel as he'd heard they were. But the worst of the lot seemed to be the half-crazed, vengeance-minded half-breed.

What had Orlo said? That they—Fred and Bright Cloud—would be saved for torturing until the chief got back? Angry Bear had a reputation among the mountain men, Fred knew. The chief was said to be the worst white-man hater in all the Rockies. And the most cunning at dealing atrocities to the human frame.

Fred recalled Muley Ballou's words on the subject, dismissed last month as the ramblings of a braggart and fool. Now Fred didn't disbelieve the most horrendous things he'd heard about his captors.

He knew he was in for the worst. He only hoped that Bright Cloud wouldn't have to suffer much more. He was responsible, after all.

Hadn't he refused to pay Brubaker's blackmail demands? And fool that he was, he thought he was lucky, and could actually make it to the Shoshone villages?

A rhythmic *thud, thud, thud* had been going on for some time, and it occurred to Fred that it wasn't his head pounding. Drums were being beaten outside. As he tried to guess the reason, he heard other sounds: the clapping of horses' hooves on the rocky ground, and a new chorus of shouts, barbaric, gleeful shouts. Fred wondered what might be the cause.

But then it occurred to him, and his blood ran cold.

Of course, the chief's war party had returned, and

Angry Bear's village could now get on with its torture-fest! *Oh, God, oh God,* the lieutenant's mind went racing. The torment of his nightmare was about to become real, in spades! For him and for Bright Cloud.

Just then the entrance flap was thrown back, and into the lodge was flung another bound white man. The fellow was bruised and covered with cuts and abrasions, his blond hair matted with dried blood, as was his swollen face with its scraggly untrimmed mustache.

Belly-down in the dirt, the arrival raised his head and looked up.

"Fred?"

"Dad?"

Tears rolled down both men's cheeks. What a time and place for their reunion!

However, the Blackfeet braves in the entrance hole were laughing and slapping each others' backs.

They looked ready to rejoin their warrior clan, get the torture blazes lit, start drinking the captured fire-water.

Thrum, thrum, thrum went the resounding drums outside. In the lodge the father sympathized with the son, and vice versa. Fred told of his and Bright Cloud's capture; the captain of his command's destruction. He finished up, "And they butchered our wounded, scalped all our dead. God! All those skinned, red-glistening soldiers' pates!"

"You were the only survivor?"

Maynard Leland wagged his head. "As a matter of

fact, no, Fred. Ballou managed to stay alive somehow, and along with me was put aboard a horse and brought here. You *do* recall Ballou, son?"

"Oh, yes. How could I forget Muley?"

Silence ensued. Then finally, "Dad, I see now how wrong I was. I shouldn't have taken Bright Cloud, left the party."

"Because you wound up here? Nonsense! *I* stayed with the party, and look at me!" The attempt at humor failed, and the men lapsed quiet again. But the captain couldn't let well enough alone. "I'm glad, Fred, that you've seen your error. No white man should marry a squaw, not under any circumstances. As for brief liaisons, they're disgusting enough, but . . ."

"Hold on!" Fred squirmed, sat up, even though it was unpleasant. His punished genitals were still aching like sin. But the least he could do was stick up for the girl. "Dad, what's *really* disgusting is your contempt for the Indian people. I never said I regretted Bright Cloud. I just wish I could've done better by her! My God, there we were in the wilderness, and me unable to defend her!" Tears were running down the young man's cheeks. "The outcome of it," he went on, "was that she got raped and put through hell. I bear the guilt for that, and perhaps worse things. For all I know, the Blackfeet may have killed her by now. No, Dad, my mistake was trying reach the Shoshones, intending to live among them! I should have married Bright Cloud at Fort Laramie, then taken her to my real home, back East."

"Home to New York? An outrageous notion, boy. *Positively* outrageous."

A thud and a loud crash, and then the warriors were crowding back into the lodge. Strong arms pulled the prisoners upright and dragged them outside.

The prisoners' unaccustomed eyes were blinded by the bright sunlight, but Orlo Brubaker's voice could be recognized, in spite of it.

"Torture time! Oh, not you gents yet, but you'll get to watch a show! Angry Bear, he's commanded that Ballou be 'tended to first. The shit's tied to a torture stake right now, and waiting."

"Oh God," groaned the Lelands in unison.

"Oh God!"

Chapter 31

Pike and McConnell hunkered in the morning shadows amid some boulders on the rim of the canyon described by Stone Badger. Down below the men spied wafting threads of smoke, but they didn't need to guess it was the village, the lodges were in plain view too. The layout was typical of Blackfeet dwelling sites, the conical tepees placed around a sizable ceremonial ground. Scores of Blackfeet warriors and squaws could be seen, plus the usual share of old folks and young 'uns.

There were also plenty of vicious-looking curs.

It was sure to be the village of Angry Bear's band. Which meant the mountain men were in range of what they sought. Fred Leland his Indian wife-to-be were down there. The only problem was, were they alive or dead?

Pike told McConnell: "Fred and Bright Cloud might be alive, but they're in trouble. Bad trouble. The Blackfeet enjoy nothing better than capturing folks, dishing out pain."

"Bad pain," Skins affirmed.

"All right, here's what we're going to do. First thing, split up again." Pike's eyes were unusually cold and steely. "I'm going down there, but you'll wait here, at least for a spell."

"Hell, Jack, it's broad daylight."

"I know it, Skins. That's why I can see *that!*" He pointed, and Skins surveyed the village more closely.

When he saw what Pike wanted him to, he husked out: "Christ!"

The ceremonial area was filling fast, and all of the Blackfeet were hurrying to take up stations. It appeared an exciting time, a festival time.

Now, what did it take to make Blackfeet enjoy themselves that way?

The realization dawned. "Jesus!"

From among the tepees some warriors were dragging the struggling figure of a man. A naked white man.

"That poor, bare-assed bastard," McConnell snorted. "Lookit! Why, they're tying him to that tall log they've gone and stuck in the ground. Jack, you can't go down there . . . Not now!"

"Think, Skins. If I don't go, and pronto, they'll start having their way with that fella, dishing out the pain. He might live a long while or he might die early, but at the very least, they'll do bad damage to his body. Now, what if that's Fred Leland?" Pike bared clenched teeth. "Look at it this way, Skins. Now *is* a damned good time to make a move. Everybody's wrapped up in celebrating. Sentries' minds won't be on lookout chores. Anyhow, I'll climb down the canyon wall, not through the mouth, where lookouts would most likely be watching.''

McConnell peered at his friend. He knew he'd lost the argument. ''All right, Jack, you'll go. And so, what'll I do?''

''Keep your eyes peeled, watch to see if I need help. I'll be prowling the village, trying to locate Fred and Bright Cloud. Maybe I'll need a diversion staged, and Skins, that's where you come in. A timely landslide, or a wildfire in the woods—you get the idea.''

''I reckon I'll go scout the canyon mouth first, picket the horses down there. Our own two, plus the Blackfoot kid's.''

''Good notion. And one other thing . . .''

Skins asked, ''What's that?''

''My Hawken, it'd be damned heavy to lug down that canyon wall. So tie it on my saddle, won't you, Skins? And keep the powder dry.''

Pike strode to the drop-off of the sheer rimrock, and as he did so checked the weapons he was keeping with him: Tomahawk, Green River knife and, heaviest of the lot, his trusty Kentucky pistol. He noticed there was little breeze, and thought it fortunate. On the precarious descent, he didn't need trouble due to wind gusts.

His moccasins were little enough protection against the sharp rocks projecting from the canyon wall. Soon his feet were tender, if not downright sore, and his hands were sustaining frequent cuts, scrapes, bruises. Not yet half-way down, bleeding fingertips became a problem. Seeking a handhold, he slipped and felt fear, so close was he to falling.

Having covered about two-hundred feet of the descent, he lost a moccasin in a crevice, but there was no choice but go on, big toe severely barked, bleeding and starting to swell. At least, he told himself, I'm most three-quarters of the way down. The worst has got to be over. Then he made another serious misstep, and a foothold crumbled away. He found himself perched between heaven and earth, then managed to leap to a nearby narrow ledge. Swiftly pushing off again, he dropped a dozen feet, groped, found a rock projection, held to it.

He took a chance of being spotted from below, took a minute or two to let quiet breathing return. Then he continued on his painstaking way down, till his feet touched the last piled shale at the foot.

There he crouched, heaving a sigh of relief.

He'd made it this far.

Now for the hard part of the escapade!

On this side of the canyon at this time of day, deep shadows were flung by the high, sheer wall. Nevertheless, it was hotter on the floor than up top, and sweat soaked Pike's buckskins, beaded his brow with salty drops. Instinct told him it was time to move, and he made plans. It seemed best to detour some miniature chimney rocks, and from there slip into the dense aspen stand. Under cover of the trees, he could make his way the hundred yards to the village outskirts.

Or so he thought.

He was scarcely among the trees when he heard a

noise, a low *chuck-chuck,* that sounded something like a human voice.

Pike stiffened and froze, paying close attention now. Drawing the tomahawk from his belt, he padded ahead stealthily in his one moccasin, the other foot bare. Tension made his palm sweat; the haft grew slippery.

From the sounds he heard, Pike reckoned a warrior had been drinking too much—drinking trade whiskey, that is. The sufferer crouched in the bushes, heaving up his stomach's contents. Should he kill the brave, taking the risk he might call out in dying? No, better to sneak on past.

With his heartbeat hammering in his ears, the mountain man slipped ahead, his feet as noiseless as possible.

Then the other warriors, waiting in the bushes, struck!

Five of them, no less.

All husky, muscle-slabbed warriors, full-grown and lusting to spill a white-man's blood.

The first burst from the shrubbery behind the mountain man, trade knife glinting in the filtered sunbeams, the sharp edge whistling as it came up, then down toward Pike. Rattlesnake-swift, Pike spun to meet the charging brave with his own bright tomahawk. The blade of the 'hawk met the brave's forehead with a *thunk,* and the Blackfoot pitched sidelong.

The warrior on his heels vented a loud, ululating yell, designed to bring still more warriors. *Now the fat's in the fire,* thought the battle-ready mountain man.

Then warriors ran at him from all compass points, their voices shrill, knives flashing and war clubs flailing.

As for Pike's plan to rescue Fred and Bright Cloud? Well, it had *seemed* a good idea, hadn't it?

Chapter 32

Pike glared about him at his charging enemies, the warlike Blackfeet, his mouth fixed in grim rictus, one big hand gripping his Green River knife, the other the tomahawk that always stood him in good stead.

Rage at the warriors who confronted him burned hotly in the mountain man's brain. He'd never been as determined to hang onto his scalp, against all odds.

Of course, he couldn't remember the odds ever being this long.

The nearest Blackfoot, a giant almost Pike's own size, charged in, muscles in his bare chest rippling, his grimacing face done half in green paint, half in black. His war club was raised for a bone-smashing blow, but Pike adroitly sidestepped and the club sliced air, not flesh.

The mountain man retaliated with a quick, hard tomahawk chop, burying the deadly blade in the Blackfoot's skull. Cranial bones shattered and pulverized brain matter flowed; the cleaved face became a blood-splashed oval, the shriek of triumph cut off in the dead brave's throat.

From Pike's right side roared out, "Yaah-hee! Yaah-hee! Die, White Eyes." The mountain man spun to see a Blackfoot, mouth twisted in a shout, rushing him. This one gripped a bow in his hands and had the arrow nocked and drawn. Pike moved with astonishing speed, diving under the flying shaft, half-falling but managing to seize his enemy.

His knife blade carved the warrior's chest and was jerked free, the Blackfoot yelping sharply, then careening down to sprawl on the turf.

The big man whirled to face the other way, but as he squared himself he was leapt at by three foes. He swiftly threw his bloodstained knife, and the blade found its mark in a brave's abdomen. While that man spun away, clutching himself, Pike yanked his Kentucky pistol, drew a bead and fired. A blossoming crimson splotch spread across the target brave's breastbone and he dropped as if poleaxed.

Pike heard the *twang* of another bowstring, and pain seared through his left leg like flame. He gave vent to a roar and grabbed his blood-leaking thigh. The place where the arrow had nicked him hurt. The mountain man staggered among the downed warriors, half-slipping on red mud, to collide with yet another wild-eyed antagonist.

Pike drove his tomahawk's blade into the man's jaw, which parted from his head, toppling him. The mountain man fell too, on top. Pike saw the life leave the Indian's face as he dropped his war hatchet, dark eyes dimming as he failed to staunch the red spill down his breadbasket.

Now Pike was completely surrounded, war cries coming from a dozen throats at once. Without weapons and beleaguered from all sides, the big man was slightly weakened but still fighting. No fewer than four braves crowded at him now, but he kicked one in the nuts, grabbing his trade knife as he fell. Pike immediately slashed open another warrior's throat and felt the man shudder as his knees collapsed. The figure hit the ground face first, his severed arteries flowing a crimson pool.

Then Pike was tackled and borne to the blood-slick earth, battered unconscious by three powerfully wielded clubs.

It was over, and Angry Bear himself strode up. The parchment-brown face frowned quizzically, then grinned.

"Ah! I know this one," cried the chief. "He-Whose-Head-Touches-The-Sky. Ah, my brothers, we'll add him to our torture orgy."

They dragged the big mountain man's slack frame toward the village center, leaping, exulting braves and squaws raising a terrific celebration.

"Tie his hands and hold him there," ordered Orlo Brubaker, known to the Blackfeet as Poison Snake. The warriors propped the woozy Pike up on his arms, and the first thing he saw on reviving was Angry Bear.

The chief lashed out with a fist, dealing a blow to the same thigh that had sustained the arrow scrape.

Pike yelped with dismay. Then the sadistic leader shoved down Pike's pants, the buckskins falling in wrinkles. The big man's large penis sagged, flaccid, until it was grabbed in an Indian's wrenching vise grip. The pain in his groin was like a thunderbolt. Pike's groin was a pit of agony, like his thigh, like his splitting head.

The gaping mountain man couldn't help but see the knife. It was in the hand of a squat squaw, wicked-eyed and leering. *Christ!* The Blackfeet women were notorious emasculators—vicious, swift and totally unmerciful!

Pike heard an ongoing gaggle of giggling, and glancing around spotted wide-eyed children looking on and laughing. But they weren't the main concern, now—that woman was. She was probably one of the chief's wives, perhaps his favorite. She certainly looked as if she held a headful of grudges—against the whites and against men in general.

Here was her chance to get even, and she looked glad as hell for it.

Pike winced as the knife-point probed his pee slit.

The chief snapped, "Go ahead, wife! Draw blood."

She twisted the blade and, sure enough, a drop leaked.

A bright red drop . . . And then another!
Jesus!

Chapter 33

Pike was sweating from every pore, the threat of losing his manhood very real, totally immediate. With cruel chief Angry Bear looking on and smirking, his torture-hungry squaw poked and prodded with her skinning knife, intent on flaying a mountain man's phallus.

But just then, an ugly character appeared wearing a coyote's head atop his own, a rattlesnake skin around his neck, a sign-decorated medicine shirt of fawn skin. The shaman performed a dance shuffle and waved his gourd rattle. "Chief. The White Eyes who were bound to the stakes earlier . . . They await!"

Angry Bear addressed his squaw. "Hold on, Swimming Fish. Let's allow He-Whose-Head-Touches-the-Sky to keep his manhood, for now. Before cutting him, we'll make him watch the other White Eyes suffer, and suffer, and suffer! And when they reach their limits and beg to be allowed to die—well, we Blackfeet will put them to still more torment!"

"You're a real piece of work, chief," bit out Pike.

"Never mind the compliments, He-Whose-Head-Touches-the-Sky! They won't buy you the release of a quick death. Come along, my warriors. And bring the White Eyes who owns the big cock that'll soon be cut off, fed to the dogs!"

With much pushing and shoving, egged on by screeching women and children who lined the way, the Blackfeet men propelled Pike through the maze of lodges toward the ceremonial ground. When they reached the grassless circle, Pike saw the peeled, scorched logs that had been set upright in the earth. To all but one of them were tied wretched, naked human beings. Cords of vine or sinew confined them by their arms, their legs and their necks.

Recognition, as well as anxiety, flashed in the captive's eyes. The bound male captives were Maynard Leland, Fred Leland and Muley Ballou. The woman with disheveled hair, bruised breasts and blood-caked thighs was Bright Cloud.

The master of ceremonies was a barrel-chested warrior with arms like wagon springs, hands like meat hooks. This was Fox-With-Foot-Missing, and he looked mean.

Mean as hell!

Pike nodded a greeting to the other captives. "Captain Leland. Lieutenant Leland and Muley. Ma'am. Good day to you folks."

"Cut the civilities, Pike," Orlo snarled. "You oughtta see you ain't in civilization. Soon as we get *you* trussed like the others, we'll start the shindig."

"If you say so, Orlo. If you say so."

None of the other prisoners said a thing, just

strained feebly at their bonds, their bleak eyes staring. As the Blackfeet tied Pike to his stake, the mountain man wondered what Skins might be up to about now.

He trusted his friend wouldn't risk his own life in a rescue attempt. Not with things so goddamned hopeless . . .

"Well, well, horse," McConnell told the big gray gelding as he drove its picket pin. "It's called letting the time pass, just like Jack said. I feel I should be down there in the canyon, but orders is orders."

So saying, he slung Pike's Hawken to the saddle bows by its thong, then let the mount crop grass. He dipped into his possibles pack for a handful of pemmican, then popped some in his mouth.

Chewed.

Songbirds chirruped in the trees, and in the grass scurried tiny stripe-backed ground squirrels. The sun was hot on the rocks down here at the canyon mouth. Reckon I'll hike back up-top, McConnell mused. Maybe Jack'll signal. Hasn't much time passed, though.

A rheumy-eyed, heavy old squaw waddled toward Muley Ballou. The scout's weathered face started to twitch and his bloodshot eyes rolled in their sockets. To Pike the man staked on the ground looked scared. Real scared.

"Atta way, Cowslip Blossom," a Blackfoot supporter called.

The encouragement was echoed, "Dig those eyes from his head!

"Slit his nose!"

"Look at him! He's a coward. Pull out his finger-nails and make him eat 'em."

While the rest of the captives were forced to watch, Ballou trembled uncontrollably. The squaw in front of him raised a flabby arm, thrust out a cactus paddle, raking the thorns down Muley's cheek. A horrified shriek burst from Muley's lips.

Christ, Pike thought. *So the poor bastard is chicken-shit. Now the redskins'll have it in for him!"*

Fox-With-Foot-Missing conferred with Angry Bear. Then, "Ho, my brothers. The old White Eyes, he fears death. Let's give him a long, drawn-out, painful one."

Brubaker hissed in Pike's ear: "You're lucky, Pike. They're gonna start with the scout, wear him down whilst you and the limp-dick sojer boys look on. That oughtta jangle your nerves, make things worse when your own time comes. This may take all day, so some of us bucks might kill time plowin' the Shoshone bitch. She don't know it, but she's a plumb hot fuck. Even reamed like she is, and with her throat screamed hoarse."

As for screams, Ballou's now filled the village center. He was cut from the stake, and thrown down roughly. Warriors led by Brown Pony spread-eagled the scout on the ground face-up, bound his wrists and ankles to stout pegs that had been driven.

His mouth working and his eyes saucering, Ballou went on screaming his fright. His tormentors were just getting warmed up. Young squaws and old old squaws were bringing burning wood chips, tossing them casually to ignite Ballou's armpit hair, chest hair, crotch hair. The scout writhed, squirmed and began to roar with real pain.

This phase lasted about an hour. And then the squaws sought different ways of amusing themselves.

While loud screams still issued in their ears, the Blackfeet women drove knives into the soles of Ballou's feet until the points speared up through the arches. Next they sawed and ripped the blades through cartilage and tendons, macerating foot flesh, amputating toes. Finally they fell back from the feebly thrashing form, laughing and chatting among themselves. Meanwhile, Pike saw, the ragged remnants of Ballou's feet flapped every which way. His legs, trembling like out-of-balance steam pistons, drummed the earth.

Then the squaws moved in again, greasy black hair glistening as their heads bowed.

The midday sun hung overhead, and the other naked captives were feeling the sting of the rays. Pike looked down at cuts and scrapes, especially the arrow slice on his thigh, and noticed that his body had turned a fiery pink.

Just then Muley let go with a loud howl of anguish. They were slowly butchering off a finger, and that was followed by another . . . and another. As shock set in, Ballou's struggles grew weaker and weaker.

But the ingenuity of the Blackfeet was great. Long hours of the afternoon spun out new thresholds of misery for Ballou, the army scout.

About mid-afternoon, Bright Cloud's bonds were cut and the woman dragged off behind a tepee. As for the guiding warriors, they made lewd gestures and clutched hard erections.

"Son of a bitch!" Skins McConnell told the sky.

No sound answered the lean, whipcord-tough mountain man. From the rimrock he could see something was wrong—very wrong—down in the Blackfeet village.

It was hard to discern precisely from this distance, but the figures in the central circle seemed changed. It looked as if three naked whites were now at the stakes, and one on the ground. Excited Indians were moving about, a parade of bucks coming and going behind a certain tepee.

What bothered McConnell was the great size of one of the bound men. Bigger than the others, it could be Jack Pike.

Now, had Jack gone and got himself captured?

If so, what could *he* do?

One possibility loomed: going down, come nightfall.

As McConnell considered options, one of his hands half-consciously dipped in his buckskins' pocket. It came out holding a small object, one of the dimpled walnut shells from the Laramie gambling fella.

Or had it come from Handy Hooper's sister? What had her name been, anyway?

Pike would recall.

Pike, who seemed to have gambled this time, and

lost disastrously. Pike, who needed rescuing in the worst way!

Skins hoped against hope his friend would be kept alive till darkness came.

He dropped the shell back in his pocket and watched a large bird coast above the canyon now.

A buzzard!

The omen wasn't a good one.

Chapter 34

As the long day finally drew to a close, the sun hovering over the western peaks in a sky of molten brass, Pike was still holding out.

Standing with broad back pressed against the thick, upright stake to which he was tied, he watched through slitted eyes the raw barbarities of the Blackfeet camp. Pike could see that the Lelands, father and son, were in bad shape—in fact, both were on the verge of emotionally cracking.

Their last twelve or more hours had been spent under extreme stress. They'd seen another human being racked with unspeakable agonies, his body mutilated in undreamed-of ways. And through it all, incredibly, Muley Ballou hadn't passed out once.

Not even when his eyes were gouged out. Not even when the skin was peeled from his scalp, exposing the bloodied skull dome. Not even when the skin bits were carved from his arms and legs, then placed in his mouth as his nostrils were pinched, forcing him to swallow.

Muley Ballou was a fool, a drinker and a rogue, Pike thought, and they'd had their differences. But he didn't deserve this.

Nobody on God's green earth deserved this.

By late afternoon the victim's screams had dwindled to faint croaks and mewings. But then, Pike saw, a fresh excitement began to ripple through the copper-skinned spectators. A new experiment in pain was about to be initiated!

As Angry Bear bestowed his cruel grin, a quartet of strong-armed squaws descended on Ballou, who hadn't writhed for several minutes. Two Blackfeet women held the victim's head, another wrenched his tongue from between his slack jaws. Then methodically, brutally, the third woman drove a stake through the tongue!

Then bringing up a knife, she began carving thin slices from Muley's pegged tongue. One after another, the slices were peeled, as if for a white man's sandwich or an Indian woman's cooking pot.

Muley Ballou bucked and jerked convulsively, and his wrists and ankles strained against his bonds. The man's scalped head thrashed on its scrawny neck. The punished scout screamed . . . and screamed . . . and screamed!

Some of the hungrier dogs began to dart in, snatch up the bloody chunks of raw meat and devour them.

Fred Leland, who'd seen it all, vomited all over himself, twitching in his own bonds.

Maynard Leland's eyes rolled back to white, and then he fainted away to hang from the stake—dead to Ballou's suffering and dead to the world.

Jack Pike was more infuriated than sickened by the gruesome show. And a bit curious over Bright Cloud's fate.

It wasn't like the Blackfeet to kill her out of sight someplace. So wasn't it likely she was still alive?

The big, tied mountain man was assuming so . . .

It was pitch dark in the village well before midnight, the moon having not yet risen. The Blackfeet had eaten supper to the tune of Muley Ballou's groans, but then had drifted off to their sleeping robes. Chief Angry Bear had proclaimed a postponement of all captive-torturing until the next day.

The biting insects were fully as bad as last night.

Pike suspected that Ballou was dead, since there'd been no movement or sound from the scout for quite a while.

"Hist!" Pike called. "Captain and Fred? Are you awake and able to palaver some?"

"I'm awake, Pike."

"So am I."

"Good. Looks like we got the night to ourselves. May as well use time to pump ourselves up, get ready for tomorrow."

Outrage tinged the captain's voice. "You have the gall to bring up tomorrow? Pike, have you no human feelings?"

Pike grinned into the darkness, although his lips were badly sunburned, like the rest of him. "Just a test, fellas, to see you've got any fight left in you. I reckon you have."

"Fat lot of good it does! These bonds are tight and we can't get loose. Damn it to hell!"

Trying to sound reassuring, Pike said: "Like a navy gent once said, 'Never give up the ship.' Lots can happen between now and sunup. Like we might get out of this fix. Climb on horses and gallop away, and to hell with Angry Bear, Brubaker and all the other nasty Blackfeet!"

"How can that possibly come about?" the captain grouched.

"Dad," Fred said, "I think I know what Pike's driving at." He wagged his head around as bonds permitted. "Bright Cloud's somewhere off in one of those lodges. She might lift a brave's knife, sneak over here and cut us loose. If that happens, we can find the band's pony herd!"

"Hmm," muttered the older officer.

"And once the ponies are located, we can steal three or four."

"Sounds like a damned long shot!"

"But a real one! Isn't that true, Pike?"

"Maybe," commented the mountain man. He wasn't ready yet to mention Skins McConnell's presence in the vicinity. Rather, he'd done some preparing of the Lelands for what might happen, while refraining from pumping their hopes too high.

A number of minutes passed in silence. Then, "Fred?"

"Yes, dad?"

"Son, the Blackfeet have been hell on us, but today I've learned something about you. You're a man, a real man, and I mean it in the best sense of the term.

209

I find myself, er, more willing now to accept your views, be not so quick to judge.''

"Dad, what are you saying?''

"Saying?'' Pike put in. "Hell, Fred, he's saying only that he saw today what I saw. That Bright Cloud is a strong, beautiful woman, able to take whatever shit the world dishes out. More able than any stuck-up, society-bred Eastern lady. And maybe, on that account, she'd make a man a fitter wife.

"I reckon, Fred,'' Pike rushed on, "that your old man, he's wanting to mend fences. Now, we don't know just now whether the Shoshone gal's alive or if she's not. But if she's alive, nobody can, or should, hold what's happened against her. She may have been embarrassed, but she's not degraded.''

"Dad, do you mean it? About the woman I'll keep wanting till my dying day?''

Maynard Leland didn't answer, because he had no chance to. Just then at the edge of the village, a shot rang out! Unless Pike missed his guess, the boom was that of a Hawken flintlock.

Pike's rope-muscled frame tensed for action. His narrowed eyes scanned the lodges and the warriors pouring out, most naked as Pike himself, and fumbling with what weapons that had come to hand when they awoke.

One piercing yell after another reached Pike's ears, apparently from over where the Blackfeets' pony herd was kept. Then a sinister, building wall of sound rolled the length of the village, in accompaniment to the shaking ground underfoot. The ponies, half-wild and spooked to panic, were off on a careening ram-page!

Skins McConnell had to be behind the stampede.

Pike, who'd been expecting something of the kind, renewed his struggles against the confining rawhide strips.

Chapter 35

As Jack Pike jerked futilely against his bonds, the Indian ponies, wild-eyed with terror, came galloping down the lanes between the lodges. Pike spied their surging haunches and flying manes silvered by the rising moon, and let out a yell of his own.

This was one of the more welcome sights he'd been treated to in a month of Sundays!

Warriors, squaws and children caught in the horses' path fell under thundering hooves or were flung back against tepees. A lanky brave waving a feathered headdress tried to turn the tide, but was run down by a wall-eyed pinto paint. Hooves crushed the fellow's rib cage.

One frenzied animal skidded to a stop and kicked out with unshod hooves. One of that day's female torturers was knocked to the earth, head slammed against a rock. Blood and brains spattered in a glistening swathe.

The entire village was engulfed in din, shouts of Indians combining with the shrieks of panicked animals. As the rampaging mounts piled into dwellings, demolishing them, they gouged themselves on split lodgepoles or tripped, breaking legs and whinnying all the more.

Warriors painted silver by the moon, fearing attack by an enemy force, nocked arrows to their bows and ran about looking for targets. A few feathered shafts were loosen at fleeting shadows—actually other Blackfeet. A mother carrying a baby saw her tiny offspring's form impaled, and a split second later felt the arrowhead in her own heart.

A large, fat elderly Indian—the village crier?—tripped over his own feet. A panicked pony fell on its side atop him, crushing his blubbery torso and punching shrieks from his throat.

At the height of the chaos came Skins McConnell, galloping his bay and leading Pike's gray, and in addition several ponies at the end of horsehair ropes. Springing from the saddle, the wiry mountain man ran to the captives, and with swift knife strokes cut them free. "Mount up Jack! You too, Leland junior and Leland senior!"

As Maynard clambered aboard a shaggy, shying roan, Pike glimpsed Fred disappearing between two lodges.

"What's eating him?"

"Bright Cloud. He's going after his woman."

"Shit, Pike, I've lit fires back there," McConnell yelled. His mount, spooked by the melee, went from fiddlefooting to downright sunfishing.

"Can't run off and leave the lieutenant," Pike grunted. "Borrow your tomahawk, Skins?" He took

213

the weapon handed to him. "Wait here or not, use your judgment, old friend. I'm going after the pair!"

Beyond the rearing cones that were the closest te-pees, a bright orange glow rose to color the night sky. As Pike ran between lodges, he was only slightly hampered by sore legs and feet. But the naked, un-protected skin of his body felt the heat of fire, a big fire, although still some distance off.

The mountain man rounded a lodge and could see now that the forest that bordered the village was ablaze. Tossing flames formed a towering burning wall. Sooty smoke billowed to the starry heavens, and the mountain man's ears filled with the great fire's cracklings.

A running figure dashed past Pike, oblivious to all but his blazing hair, blazing buckskins. Then, more to the big man's interest, he spotted Fred. "Over this way, Pike. I've got Bright Cloud with me, but she's hurt!"

"Hold on, Fred. Be right with you."

Super-heated pitch droplets from the burning pines pelted the sprinting, naked mountain man. But be-tween him and Leland and his woman, another Black-foot warrior leaped. The panting buck clutched a war club that *whooshed* as he swung it.

The mountain man's heart was beating like a Chey-enne war drum. As Pike and the Blackfoot came to-gether, he rammed an elbow into the painted brave's chest. As the warrior gasped for breath, Pike fol-lowed his first belt with a kick in the testicles that sent the enemy rolling on fallen pine needles.

Pike reached down and plucked the war club out

214

of the dirt. Now he clutched both a tomahawk and the club. Naked Fred Leland, lanky hair flying, had nearly reached him now, dragging along the nude, limping Bright Cloud. But two painted braves were rushing to intercept the pair, their faces lit by flames from the lodges!

"Ho! There's He-Whose-Head-Touches-the-Sky, the hated one!"

"You kill him, my brother! I'll take the wagging-pecker White Eyes!"

The fiercely scowling warriors reached for their knives, but it was already too late. Pike powered toward them on surging legs, taking on one foe with a hard-swung tomahawk blow to the shoulder, after which the damaged arm dangled grotesque and loose. Next a backhanded swipe with the club obliterated the brave's eye socket, at the same time killing him.

At the same moment, Pike heard a menacing laugh ring out, "Good-bye, Long Knife!"

The other brawny brave had drawn back his knife to stab Fred. Bright Cloud had been pushed to the ground, where she lay panting. Pike threw himself at the attacker, bowling into him like a loose cannon on a frigate's gun deck.

The two battlers tumbled to the ground, where they rolled over and over, then came to rest with Pike on top.

Attempting desperately to drive his blade up into Pike while lying on his back, the brave was surprised when the mountain man vised his wrist and bent his arm backward . . . backward. The move reversed the cant of the razor-sharp cutting edge, and put Pike's considerable weight behind it.

The blade buried itself between the Blackfoot's ribs. The face of Crow Hawk became a chalky death mask.

"On your feet, Fred! On your feet, Bright Cloud! My pard Skins, he's got horses waiting."

"How's dad?"

"Must be wishing you'll get your ass hustling. Now, damn it, *git!*"

Under the pelting of fireballs from the burning lodges they ran, the threesome seeing Skins, Maynard and the horses at the end of the lane amid a conflux of flame and smoke. Injured Blackfeet raised a clamor of screams, endangered men and women ran about in panic as the blaze devoured their homes. Charred buffalo hides and lodgepoles, dead horses and people littered the village.

Pike, Fred and Bright Cloud burst through the smoke curtain, air hotter than a furnace searing aching lungs. Twenty yards to the horses . . . fifteen yards . . . then ten . . .

In front of the big mountain man sprang Orlo Brubaker, and the man clutched a musket. "Goddamn you, Pike! You done this, just when my revenge was gonna be complete."

The heavy gunbarrel came up and stared Jack Pike squarely in the eye. But with lightning speed the enraged mountain man swept aside the barrel, leveled a terrific tomahawk chop to the half-breed's face.

The man with two names, Brubaker and Poison Snake, reeled back, and Pike felt his hand and arm splashed with a cascade of warm liquid. The half-breed's eyes popped with shock above his frightful, blood-gushing wound. Pike jumped to one side as the man fell and frantically kicked his life away.

The mountain man didn't wait for the blood to spread and pool, but sprinted toward his horse.

Fred and Bright Cloud were already mounted and ready to ride. Maynard and McConnell, mounted too, had handed them some scorched wolf hides plucked from a wrecked tepee. They'd used them to cover naked hips and loins.

Pike vaulted to the saddle. "Ride, everybody! Ride!" the big man shouted.

He, McConnell, Bright Cloud and the two Lelands started galloping headlong. In a minute they were out of the village.

In two minutes more they were through the canyon gap.

Epilogue

When the lemon sun rose in the sky to the east, Pike reined the gray gelding in on the trail. He peered across at his companions, their only clothing—except for McConnell—were saggy kilts of wolf skin. Everybody looked happy, though. Damned happy.

They were alive, after all.

"Well, folks, what now?"

Expressions turned perplexed.

Pike bit out a few terse statements. "Look, you two Lelands, as for the map party, it's wiped out. You men have your army obligations, true, but they can wait—or so I'm thinking. What our gang needs now is two things. clothes and rest." He glanced at McConnell and winked. "Well-l-l, *maybe* more than two things."

Fred spoke up. "Can't we head for the Shoshone lands? Bright Cloud's People?"

Pike responded: "My thoughts, exactly."

Bright Cloud put in, "Shoshone women, they *do* know how to make guests welcome in camp!"

"I know," Pike said.

"I know," Skins said.

"Har*rumph*," muttered Leland, senior. "Gentlemen, it's been years since I've taken the opportunity to . . ." His face grew as red as his sunburned chest. "Er, I'm a widower, you see."

Pike, grinning in his wolf skin, nudged McConnell with a bare elbow. "Maybe that's partly where your problem lies, Captain. From time to time a man plain gets to needing a woman. It's only natural. Just ask Fred."

For the first time since daylight, the captain's gaze went unabashedly to the woman. Her breasts jutted proudly, and her eyes were clear. He lowered his hand to screen the bulge under his wolf skin.

"Pike, I think you may be right."

"I *know,* I'm right, Maynard."

"Let's get a move on, folks," McConnell said. "Three days, and we'll be in good ol' Buffalo Tail's village."

Pike gave the cavalry "forward-ho" signal.

They rode.

THE END

FOR THE BEST OF THE WEST, SADDLE UP WITH PINNACLE AND JACK CUMMINGS . . .

DEAD MAN'S MEDAL	(664-0, $3.50/$4.50)
THE DESERTER TROOP	(715-9, $3.50/$4.50)
ESCAPE FROM YUMA	(697-7, $3.50/$4.50)
ONCE A LEGEND	(650-0, $3.50/$4.50)
REBELS WEST	(525-3, $3.50/$4.50)
THE ROUGH RIDER	(481-8, $3.50/$4.50)
THE SURROGATE GUN	(607-1, $3.50/$4.50)
TIGER BUTTE	(583-0, $3.50/$4.50)

WALK ALONG THE BRINK OF FURY:

THE EDGE SERIES

Westerns By GEORGE G. GILMAN

PINNACLE BOOKS HAS
SOMETHING FOR EVERYONE—

MAGICIANS, EXPLORERS, WITCHES AND CATS

THE HANDYMAN (377-3, $3.95/$4.95)

He is a magician who likes hands. He likes their comfortable shape and weight and size. He likes the portability of the hands once they are severed from the rest of the ponderous body. Detective Lanark must discover who The Handyman is before more handless bodies appear.

PASSAGE TO EDEN (538-5, $4.95/$5.95)

Set in a world of prehistoric beauty, here is the epic story of a courageous seafarer whose wanderings lead him to the ends of the old world—and to the discovery of a new world in the rugged, untamed wilderness of northwestern America.

BLACK BODY (505-9, $5.95/$6.95)

An extraordinary chronicle, this is the diary of a witch, a journal of the secrets of her race kept in return for not being burned for her "sin." It is the story of Alba, that rarest of creatures, a white witch: beautiful and able to walk in the human world undetected.

THE WHITE PUMA (532-6, $4.95/NCR)

The white puma has recognized the men who deprived him of his family. Now, like other predators before him, he has become a man-hater. This story is a fitting tribute to this magnificent animal that stands for all living creatures that have become, through man's carelessness, close to disappearing forever from the face of the earth.